HOOKED ON HER

ICE KINGS SERIES, #3

STACEY LYNN

Hooked On Her

Ice Kings, #3

Stacey Lynn

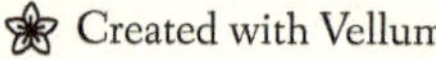 Created with Vellum

CHAPTER ONE

Tessa

"WHAT THE HELL?"

My purse hits the floor with a *thunk* and behind me, the closing of my apartment door echoes.

At least, I'm pretty sure I'm in my apartment. The same one I've lived in for three years with my recently ex-fiancé, Will.

We broke up weeks ago, although I should have kicked his butt out much sooner. I'm either a descendant of a reptile with the matching cold heart, or I'm confident in my decision to end things because I don't miss him.

My fingers curl around my keys, my only line of defense, although from what I can see, there's nothing left to steal or take because there's *nothing* in my living room. Not our couches or our small TV stand or our television. The only evidence my furniture was ever here are the imprints in the carpet and edges of a slight dust stain around where bookshelves and couches went unmoved for years.

My pulse skyrockets and for a moment I think to call Will. I've been calling him for weeks to come get his stuff and clear it out. Preferably while I was working. My last message a few days ago was well past the point of rude.

"Listen here, coke-sniffing probably homeless asshole. Get your crap out of my apartment this weekend when I'm out of town or when I get back, it's all getting tossed in the dumpster. I mean it, Will."

It only makes sense I was robbed after he left the place unlocked, key on the counter, and then it was raided after he hauled away the only things he should have taken—like his clothes, because everything else was bought by *me*. There's no way Will came and cleaned out his things and mine. Is there?

I do a thorough search of the apartment, senses tingling in my fingertips, driving me toward the kitchen first. I expect to open a cabinet and see my dishes, pale blue with yellow stripes around the edges stacked nicely next to the matching bowls. But nope. Gone. In fact, all the cupboards are emptied except for some canned vegetables.

"Seriously?" I open and then slam the pantry door shut. Even our dry goods are gone. Plus the opened bottle of wine I'd left on the counter the other night. What monster takes an opened bottle of wine?

Every guest room closet and bathroom cupboard are emptied in the exact same way and as I grow closer to our bedroom, fury spins itself into a heavy and thick knot in my stomach.

I can't believe he's done this to me. Loser. That's what he is. He didn't used to be one, or he had me so fooled to not imagine he could become this guy but I still can't believe he was able to snowball me this hard. When we met, Will

Stantham was a personal banker with Toronto Royal. He worked three floors above me, managing millions of dollars of assets while I sat in a cubicle at our headquarters, mindlessly helping design pamphlets and slogans for marketing campaigns.

A marketing assistant for a bank. Not exactly the high-energy or creative work I hoped for when I stepped foot into what I anticipated would be an exciting world of marketing and advertising.

Then things changed. He missed out on a promotion, got pissy and insubordinate with his boss, eventually he was let go and struggled to find a new job. Through it all, for the last year, I've been nothing but supportive until I couldn't be anymore. I've covered for him, watched as he lost weight, stayed up all hours of the night, and then slept for days.

I'm not an idiot. At some point, he started using drugs. The white powder on my coffee table wasn't even the first clue that showed something wasn't right. It was, however, the final straw.

But this?

"How kind of him," I mutter, kicking the carry-on suitcase he's left me with. It's the reason I returned to the apartment this afternoon.

I have a flight to catch.

But now... should I even go? I scan the apartment and let out a laugh. It bounces off the walls before I cringe at the sound of my maniacal laughter. It's either go see my brother or spend the weekend sleeping in a hotel. The bastard didn't even have the manners to leave me my bed. And I just bought it two months ago. I knew I should have bought two twin beds instead of a king. It's not like we've shared our bed in months anyway.

I tug on the handle to the suitcase and blow out a breath. My thoughts are scattered. I should call the police. Report Will. But maybe it's not him? Does renter's insurance cover this?

My mind swirls as I release the handle of my suitcase. Regardless of my next move, I can't stay here. There's nothing but salad and floors that need to be vacuumed, and no vacuum.

Figures. Will hasn't cleaned the apartment in three years, but he steals the vacuum? To what, pawn it?

I can't wrap my head around this.

As if he knows my struggle, because Sawyer and I have always been able to read each other's moods better than a dollar store mood ring, my phone starts belting out the lyrics to "*Whatta Man*" circa 1993 Salt-N-Pepa. He despises it when I sing it to him every time he does something nice for me.

And as his little sister, my job is to drive Sawyer to certifiable insane levels.

I rush to the muted lyrics coming from my phone where I dropped my purse and grab it, hitting the talk button before I miss his call.

"Sawyer," I say, breathless.

"What's wrong?" He has somehow honed his mind-reading capabilities from twelve hundred plus kilometers.

His voice is a boom. I can picture his scowl. Black brows, thicker than mine mostly because he'd rather have his balls chopped off than step into a salon, are most likely yanked together.

"I..." The shock of what I've stepped into hits me like a two by four to the stomach. And that hurts. Sawyer did it to me once when I was twelve. He still claims it was an accident. I still remember him doubled over in laughter. "I..."

"Tessa. Damn it. Talk to me."

Patience isn't his strength.

Tears well and fall down my cheeks, dribble off my chin before I can stop them. "Sawyer," I cry. "Something happened. My place... I think Will took everything."

He curses like I'm his opponent on the ice, smack-talking my ex, and then he does what he always does.

He takes control, looks after me and does his job as big brother—he protects me and helps me when everything goes sideways.

Hours later, I'm a grimy mess after shuffling through customs, waiting for the plane, and sitting crammed in the middle seat of a full flight.

But then I'm wrapped in my big brother's rib-crushing hug, my face burrowing into his chest.

"Hey, sis."

I sniff, probably leaving a snot stain across his T-shirt. I'll point it out later when I'm in the mood to laugh.

"Sawyer," I groan. It's possible I'm trying to claw my way into my brother's embrace. I stink. My hair is a greasy mess and I need a six-pack of beer and a huge plate of nachos to forget this day.

"Hey. I love you, but you fuckin' reek."

I slap his shoulder and pull back, wiping my finger under my nose and then swipe it beneath my other snot stain on his shirt.

"Gross." He smacks my hand away and then grabs my chin. He cringes at it and I shove him again, laughing.

"You suck."

"You smell like a dumpster."

"It's the plane. Should have bought me a better ticket."

Laughter aside, I feel better, but the ugliness of the day is still there, weighing me down.

"You okay? Serious."

"I don't know. About ending things with Will, well, I was... until today. But *everything* is gone."

My artwork. My books. Journals I wrote in when I was a teenager and saved in a box. What kind of jerk does that? He took every single thing from our apartment except for a few crumbs of lint fuzz. What's the point he's trying to make?

And *why?*

"Then it's a good thing you're here." He throws his arm over my shoulders and pulls me to him. With the ease of a guy who travels weekly during the season, he grabs my suitcase and ushers me through the crowd of the Charlotte airport and out to the short-term parking lot.

"Where's Debbie?" Usually she comes with, screeching and squealing and throwing her arms around me possibly tighter than Sawyer's grip.

"She's uh... she's not feeling well." His jaw tightens and his hand scrubs his shoulder-length brown hair. He's in need of a haircut but his hockey team's pre-season starts next week. Sawyer won't cut his hair until the season's over whether that's in early April or well after if the Ice Kings make it to the playoffs.

"Not feeling well?"

"Just a bug. Or something. She'll be fine. She's excited to see you, though."

"Anyone else?" I hate that I ask. I hate I always ask about him. I've had a crush on my brother's best friend since before I could drive a car. It's embarrassing and a habit I've tried to kick, but it's no use. Jason Taylor is firmly cemented in my brain as the most perfect guy in existence and no one else measures up.

"I'm sure Jason can't wait to see you, too."

"Right." I doubt it. Jason barely talks to me anymore and when he does, it's usually with both of us sharing tight-lipped verbal barbs to see who will walk away first.

Usually, it's me. Except on New Year's. Jason did the walking away then.

Stop! I shout to myself silently. New Year's Eve was a mirage. I'm certain he didn't brush my hair off my shoulder, skim his lips across my cheek and linger, whispering, *"You'll find the guy for you who deserves you when you're ready to open your eyes."*

Oddly enough, I'd been plastered against a dark hallway, eyes closed as he spoke, and when I did manage to pry them open... the hallway was empty.

But no. I've convinced myself that night was one of my many dream-induced fantasies I've created over the years starring my brother's teammate, one of the best wingers in professional hockey.

Please. He can have any woman. He doesn't need his best friend's little sister.

And the fact he still only sees me as a little sister is part of the reason why I'm so angry around him. I'm aware enough to realize it.

"You know," Sawyer says, lifting my suitcase into the back of his Tundra with ease. "I still can't figure it out. Jason gets along with everyone and yet somehow, you two can't be in a room together without me needing to hide the knives."

Well, you see, big brother, when you fall in love with a guy six years older than you and spend years trying to find someone to replace him because you can't get over the fantasy version you've created for yourself, it makes you a wee bit sassy in his presence.

No big deal, really.

That's right... hours ago, Will emptied my apartment and stole everything from me, and it's all Jason Taylor's fault. I can trace that web of ridiculous thought all the way back to him one thin, silken strand at a time.

CHAPTER TWO

Tessa

I SHOVE A TOASTED bagel into my mouth and chew slowly. Hard to force food down when the sound of retching can still be heard down the hall. I'm not certain if my brother still thinks I'm a naive nine-year-old, but if he does, he's a bigger idiot than I usually think he is.

A behemoth on the ice. A dolt in person.

It doesn't take a genius to figure it out. Yesterday, Debbie had a bug. She was fine when I got here and then passed out on the couch at eight o'clock. I woke this morning to the sound of her throwing up, her laughing, throwing up again, and Sawyer's murmurs through the wall —apparently their bathroom is on the other side of my bedroom—telling her she only has a few more weeks to go.

Whether they're hiding it from me because of everything that's happening with Will, or they're waiting to tell the team and family until she's past the first trimester is the only question I have.

And it better not have anything to do with me.

The heavy thud of Sawyer heading down their wood staircase draws my attention from my spot in their open kitchen and I grin as Sawyer saunters toward me. He's showered, dressed in his athletic gear. I'm assuming he's headed to the team's practice facility for a workout. As a defenseman for the Ice Kings, and with their season starting soon, if I know my brother, he's in full-on, last minute, kick ass on the ice mode twenty-four seven.

Or at least he usually would be, if he didn't look like he was getting ready to puke himself.

I snort and chomp down on my bagel.

He glances at me and heads to the coffee pot.

"When is she due?" I ask. There's no point in beating around the bush.

He curses and I laugh. Coffee drips down his wife-beater tank top and he's swiping at his crotch.

"Damn it, Tess. Don't startle me like that."

I swivel on my stool and cross my arms. "She has a bug." I use finger quotes and he glares at me. "She was comatose on the couch by eight last night and she and I usually stay up until one in the morning drinking wine, which by the way, I noticed she didn't touch, and then she's been puking all morning. I'm single and Canadian, Sawyer. Not an imbecile."

He rips off paper towels from the holder next to the sink and keeps cleaning his pants. Wadding them into a ball, he tosses them at the garbage can near me.

He misses by a long shot.

"Nice." I slide off the stool and toss them inside. "Are you keeping it a secret from everyone or just me?"

He huffs and takes his second turn at his coffee. This time I wait until he's done. Making him spill once was an accident, if I do it again, he'll probably toss his mug at my face.

"Debbie wants to wait until she's passed the first trimester." He glances down the hall before lowering his voice and returning to me. "She's only eight weeks. Sick all the time."

His coffee mug trembles in his hand. It rattles like my heart and while I logically *knew* my brother's long-term girlfriend was pregnant, as it settles in and he confirms, my emotions take over.

My brother is going to be a dad. Hell. *I'm going to be an aunt!*

"Sawyer!" I screech, shove to my feet, and I throw myself at him. The move makes coffee slosh over the rim, his stomach, and pants again and this time I end up as soaked as him. "This is so exciting!"

"You're such a brat," he groans and shoves me back. "Why are you doing this to me?" He brushes his hand down his shirt and drips of coffee fly into the air before splattering onto his white tile floor.

"Sorry."

"No. You're not."

"A little." I shrug. "I'm more happy than anything, though."

"Yeah." His smile wavers before he points a finger at me. "Two steps away. I want a cup of my own damn coffee before I'm wearing all of it."

I raise my hands and step back, questions bubble. They've been dating for years and have lived together for two.

And now they're having a baby.

"Was this... was this planned?" I ask.

"No." The mug in his hand shakes again and I laugh. I

haven't seen my brother nervous since, well... ever. Even when he was in college and knew he was going to be drafted, he didn't tremble.

I'm itching to give him crap for it but in truth, his nerves make me nervous.

"Are you... are you okay with this?"

"What? Yeah. Yeah, of course I'm okay with it." He shoves a hand through his dark hair and makes a face. Not a good one. "It's just... we're not married. Or engaged. And I thought we had more time but now..."

He trails off. My heart pinches. "Sawyer. If you want to marry her, all you have to is ask her."

He sets down his coffee mug and sighs, taking one more glance down the hall. "I don't want her to think I'm asking because she's pregnant. Like I'm, I don't know, only asking because it's what I should do."

See? He's such a dolt!

A laugh bubbles so fiercely and quickly I can't contain it to which he scowls at me.

I slide the plate of crackers toward him that I'd prepared earlier, laughing even harder. "She's been in love with you for years and lives with you. She would have said yes to marrying you three nights after you met, you idiot. Just ask her. Oh, and take her crackers. If she keeps some by her bed, it'll help with morning sickness."

"How do you know?" His tone is suspicious, borderline angry.

I roll my eyes. "Because I have female co-workers who have had babies. Don't glare at me like that. Go, take care of your girl, and grow some balls on the trip to her."

"You're a brat."

"Love you too, Soy-sauce."

He growls at me and I jump out of the way. When I was

little, I couldn't pronounce his name correctly, so I shortened it to soy. Then I learned about soy sauce and started calling him that when he was a teenager. I loved the pissy face he made when he had his high school girlfriends over and I called him that.

I'm halfway back to my room, trying to figure out what I'm going to do for the day. By my count, I only have a couple of hours before Debbie's feeling better, Sawyer digs his balls and guts out of a hidden corner, and then they're celebrating.

And I've already learned how thin the walls are here.

"Hey!" he calls out and I spin on my heels.

"Yeah?"

"You still coming to Jude's Labor Day party Monday?"

"Wouldn't miss it!"

Normally I'd mean it. Today I'm lucky my voice doesn't crack from the lie.

I usually love every opportunity to be around Sawyer's team but this weekend, I feel more like hibernating. Except I don't even have time for that. I have to start figuring out what in the hell I'm going to do to get my stuff back. I'm not exactly up for a round of partying with my brother's friends, their happy girlfriends and wives, and pretending my life hasn't exploded in the last twenty-four hours.

Back in my room, I grab my phone and earbuds. I throw my hair up into a ponytail and tug on my running shoes. Sawyer doesn't live far from Freedom Park. Getting out of his house while he figures out what to do with Debbie is my first priority, compiling a to-do list of what I have to deal with when I return to Toronto next week my second, and third... running until I forget all about the fact that in another forty-eight hours, I'm going to have to face Jason Taylor... and see if what happened on New

Year's was my overactive drunken imagination. Or a reality.

And I have no idea how I'll handle either circumstance.

"EXCUSE ME?" I'm huffing. I no longer know if it's from exertion from my run or the phone call that slammed into me like we're professional wrestlers and my back just hit the mat.

"If you want, we're happy to close the account, issue new cards."

I laugh. "What good will closing the account do? There's nothing left!"

Mothers with young children shove their little ones to the far right side of the running path. *That's right, perfectly done up mothers in athleisure wear, move along, ignore the crazy Canadian.*

Ha. Oh my God. I am losing my mind.

I throw my hand in the air and illicit several strange looks. It has to be from my screech. Perhaps I look rabid. I know I certainly *feel* rabid. If freaking cokehead Will were standing in front of me, I'd tear him apart with my teeth.

"You're kidding me, right?" I spin, shove my hand through my hair and yank out my ponytail. My mass of brown hair flies every which way and into my teeth. I yank it out, spitting.

"Ew," a woman says, scrunching her face with disgust and hurrying her steps.

Awesome. I'm now spitting on strangers. Perhaps there's foam in my mouth.

Maybe I really do have rabies.

I'm usually polite. Canadians pride ourselves on our

politeness and manners. I have no time for the woman who's glaring at me over her shoulder once again before dawdling toward the parking lot.

"I assure you, Miss Chauncy. This is no joke. However, I can freeze everything until you decide what you want to do."

What I want to do is find Will and slit his throat. *Wow, there, Tessa. Let's take a hop, skip, and a jump back to saneville, k, sweetie?*

My subconscious crouches low so as not to startle me, wiggling her fingers delicately so I can cross an actual white painted line. I imagine it as the outline of Will's body and step toward it.

I need to stop watching so many thriller movies ASAP. The last thing I need is to end up in jail. Which really, puh-lease.

There's not a jury who will convict. I'll explain every-thing, represent myself without an attorney since I can't even pay for one because hahahahaha, Will has stolen *everything!*

"Yesterday was payday," I mumble, firmly aware the person on the phone from fraud security does not give a shit about my payday or my problems. They can fake it with the best of them with their caring tones but they make less than I do. They definitely don't make nearly enough to deal with the mental breakdown of a team member. "My rent is due soon. And I'm out of the country. I mean, holy shit. My savings, too?"

"Yes, ma'am."

The urge to snap so she does not call me ma'am again rises and I firmly push it down. It's not Allison's fault my ex is a gianter douche than I originally thought. Gianter isn't even a word. Great. He's reduced me to forgetting basic English.

"Close the accounts," I whisper. My fury is lodged in my throat and my voice sounds scratchy. Ruined. I've spent the last year allowing Will to slowly ruin our relationship when I knew deep down I should have ripped the band-aid off a long time ago... hello! There was coke residue on my coffee table!

Or, make that his coffee table now.

My knees buckle and I hurry off the pavement to a nearby bench. There, I drop my head into my hand and swear into the phone.

"Close the account," I repeat. "Cancel the cards immediately. And thank you for letting me know."

"Yes ma'am." The rep clears her throat. "You'll be okay."

"Yeah. Thanks, Allison."

"You're welcome. Enjoy your weekend."

I hang up, letting loose another hysterical laugh. "Enjoy your weekend!" I cry out, falling back onto the bench. "She told me to enjoy my weekend!"

"Excuse me. Miss?"

I crack open one eye and then another. In front of me is an elderly gentleman, haggard beard that covers the front of his collar of his button-up shirt. He's thin, wearing a fishing hat and holding two fishing poles. He has a slight hunch to his shoulders like the weight of the world has worn him down over the years.

Oh buddy, I can relate. I'm pretty sure I saw him casting earlier and waved happily to him on my run... before the phone call.

Before my sanity splintered.

"Yes?"

"Life has a way of kickin' you when you're already down, doesn't it?"

"Yeah. You could say that."

"Want to know what I've learned in all my eighty-four years of walkin' this earth?"

No. No, I do not need sage advice from an underweight Santa Claus. But I'm a polite Canadian. "Sure. Hit me with it."

"Good news is when you think you're at your lowest, and you feel like you look like right now, the only way to go is up."

He tips his hat and waves. I glare at him until he disappears between two parked pickup trucks.

Did that strange, nice man just say I look like shit?

Yep. Yep, he did.

I suppose that confirms what he's said... I've officially hit the lowest of my lows in the lowliest parts of the dredges I ever thought I could go.

Enjoy my weekend indeed.

CHAPTER THREE

Tessa

I'M RIGHT where I've wanted to be since I was eighteen years old and really started imagining what sex would be like. And he's here.

Jason Taylor. Broad-shouldered, strong chest, abs that aren't bricks but carry a layer of weight on top. It shows his strength every time he rolls his hips.

And he's a *master* at rolling his hips.

What will it feel like when he's inside of me?

Soon. So soon. I'm desperate for this. This moment. With him. Us. I'm taking a page out of the feminist playbook and I am *persisting* toward the goal I've had for years.

Jason Taylor, taking something I've only ever wanted him to have.

"Please," I gasp as I wrap my hand around his length. He's so strong and large and perfect everywhere, but a shiver wracks my spine. This will *fit?* Logically, yes. I've taken health classes. I've had anatomy. My senior year of high school I thought I wanted to be a nurse, so I took a program through the high school. Physically, he will fit.

Emotionally? *Wow.*

"Tessa." My name sounds like it's been scratched over sandpaper on the way out of his mouth. He's tense, holding himself above me while his fingers slide to an area that hasn't been used outside my own hands in way too long. I spread my legs wider and when he presses one finger inside me, I arch into him.

Oh God... yes. After all these years we're really doing this and it is *so freaking good.*

I'm already so close. My body is trembling. And my hands slide over his chest, curl around his shoulders as he works me quickly, never once taking his dark brown eyes off me.

"Please," I whimper again and tighten my grip on his hard length. His head falls down and his long hair makes me lose sight of his dark brown eyes. He's dark and tan everywhere.

North Carolina agrees with him.

"Jesus. We shouldn't be doing this, Tess."

I wrap my legs around his thighs and pull him toward me.

"I want this." I don't care that I already know it won't last beyond this one night.

I know him well enough.

I'm still going for it.

To prove how much I want him, I reach for the night-stand. He's already thrown a strip of condoms onto it and I tear one off, handing it to him.

"Are you doing it or am I?"

Look at me, being brave. He eyes me again, condom in one hand, foil packet in the other. His chest heaves. I press my hand to the hair on his chest. I like he's not manscaped and instead *all man*. His hair is coarse, brushes over one pec, to the other, down the center and out to the sides.

"You have no idea how long I've wanted this, Tessa."

"Same. For as long as I can remember." I dig my hand into his bicep, pulling him to me. "Kiss me and fuck me, Jason."

"Shit. So fucking sexy," he groans against my mouth.

My feminine wiles do a back handspring. He thinks I'm sexy!

I feel his hand move between us, and my fingers tangle in his hair, holding him against me. And then he's there, right *there*, where he's already been and prepared me but I still brace for him.

"Tessa—" His hand is still wrapped around his dick and his mouth is brushing against mine.

"I want you."

"I don't want to hurt you."

Guaranteed he'll hurt me. I'm also pretty sure he's not referring to my vagina. Seriously. He's BIG.

"You won't. You can't."

"Sure?" His hand strokes his dick. I look down and *wow* it's hot watching him touch himself.

"Ye—"

"Any way you want it, that's the way you need it!"

I bolt up in bed, sweat drips down my forehead and I flip my hand to my heart as my alarm continues to blare.

And oh! Ha ha ha. Prophetic, Journey. You've got me. It was definitely the way I needed it.

"Any way you want it, that's the way you need it!" Okay, Journey, enough of this madness. I slap the alarm app on my phone, pulse pounding louder than the music.

This is ridiculous. Absolutely ridiculous. Only a lunatic

has *sex dreams* starring her brother's best friend who in all the years of knowing each other has never once, never a single darn time, acted like he has any feelings for me outside being a family member.

I really need to consider getting some help with this. It can't continue. I don't know if it was what he said on New Year's, which I'm still not convinced is real... or if it's the fact I'm single for the first time in years. But this is enough.

It's time to put this crush to bed. Not like the bed I just dreamed about having him in though. Although, it *is* a comfortable bed. For a moment, the dream resurfaces and my body warms.

"No. Stop it, you moron." I slap my forehead and groan.

My groan echoes, like it's coming through the walls and I scowl at the cream painted wall. That second one isn't from me.

I lift my head, peering at the wall I know shares its placement with my brother's bathroom. The same bathroom where Debbie spent most of the other morning puking up her guts.

This... this is not a morning sickness groan. It's not an any kind of sickness groan.

Another muffled sound.

Laughter.

Oh God. I might be the one puking if I have to hear my brother and his girlfriend going at it any more.

"Sick." I shove off the bed, fling the covers up toward the pillows at the headboard. I dress in record time, mostly because there's a countdown to completion coming from the wall. The sounds are louder. Something keeps banging and echoing. I'm running down the hall and then the stairs to the kitchen, hands over my ears to stave off any louder sounds I might hear in the hallway.

After I inhale a quick package of raspberry yogurt, I head out. Another run sounds like the best way to start the day.

Heck, staying with Sawyer for longer than a weekend might be a great decision for me. How else am I going to get in such kick-ass shape than these frequent runs?

Besides, there's nothing else for me to do until it's time to go to the pool party later. It's a holiday weekend. By the time I got my act together on Saturday after talking to my bank, all the other offices I thought to call were closed for the weekend. I can't do a darn thing until Tuesday except make lists of what I need to do to fix this stupid situation with Will and my apartment. I mean, I've paid rent early, but payday isn't for another two weeks. It's not like I'm swimming in money and he's stolen everything. What do I do? Buy an air mattress and camp out in my apartment until I can slowly replace everything I spent years setting up?

The easiest thing would be to ask Sawyer for help. A couple thousand dollars for rent and some help refurnishing my apartment is nothing to him. If I ask though, he'll hand me ten times what I need and refuse to be paid back. Then I'll be left indebted to him.

I've worked hard in my life to figure out how to be successful on my own. My parents and I don't lean on my brother. His millions are his because he's earned them with sacrifice and his own sweat, tears, and blood. Literally. Hockey's a violent sport.

The only thing I accepted from Sawyer, ever, is the small sedan he bought me on my twenty-first birthday.

This time, I might need his help.

But I'll only take it after I exhaust every single other possible option.

CHAPTER FOUR

Tessa

THE FIRST TIME Jason came home with Sawyer, I was dressed in my cheerleading outfit, pompoms in hand and my backpack in the other. I'd just gotten home from school and had barely enough time to eat before I had to get to the game. At some point in my earlier ages, I prohibited all things hockey from entering my life. I stopped going to my brother's games because I was tired of spending every single weekend and many weeks during the summer being freezing cold, sitting my butt on metal bleachers, sipping hot chocolate while my parents and everyone around them talked about how awesome and amazing Sawyer Chauncy is.

Unfortunately, the only way to get out of going to games was to be busy with something else. So I took dance. I joined lacrosse... and then quickly quit after taking a stick to the boob. Yowch. No amount of padded sports bra could ever make me want to relive that throbbing pain again.

I would wonder if Sawyer and I were even blood related if we didn't have the same stubborn attitude and quick-witted and dry sense of humor. We look nothing alike, he's all dark and broody to my lighter features. And when it comes to athletic abilities... he got all of it.

I'm pretty sure my parents had his DNA adjusted in utero and then when it came to me, they said, "Nah, we already have one phenomenally talented kid, mediocre will do for number two."

Fortunately for me, our basketball team sucked and rarely had fans in the stands, so it was easy to make the cheerleading squad. I didn't care that no one cheered along, that occasionally we were booed while trying to cheer, and that one time, the visiting team with packed stands and the kind of crowd most basketball teams died for took pity on us and cheered along with us... the competitor's team cheer-leaders.

Talk about humiliating.

Still, between cheerleading and finding a job waiting tables at a small diner in town when I turned sixteen, it meant I was no longer subjected to weekend traveling with my family.

Don't get me wrong. I love them. I always have and I always will, and Sawyer is one of my best friends. I don't blame him for seeing me as the sidepiece. I don't blame him for the fact that our mom had me cooking meals as soon as I turned twelve because they were so busy running Sawyer to practice and tournaments. It's not Sawyer's fault I did his laundry and mine because he was never home.

It *is* Sawyer's fault for ever coming home with Jason Taylor, the boy with the hazelnut brown eyes and dark black hair that swayed and curled around the tips of his ears and the collar of his shirt. It is Sawyer's fault for getting a kick out of teasing me in my cheerleading gear right as I grabbed sight of possibly the world's sexiest man alive.

There he was, standing across the kitchen from me next to my brother, shoving a potato chip into his mouth, looking drop-dead gorgeous while doing it.

My jaw dropped, my knees went weak, and I tripped over an uneven tile in my parents' kitchen floor, slamming my forehead into a corner of their kitchen countertop. I quickly looked like every teenage girl in a horror film with blood gushing down my face, screams piercing the air, and the cheerleader outfit to really seal the deal.

In my defense, I'm still willing to bet that the screams were from Sawyer. He's always been squeamish at the sight of blood. Which meant it was Jason who scooped me into his arms like every romance hero in every novel I've ever read and whisked me away to safety—er... the emergency room, on his brilliant, strong steed... or my brother's rented Suburban. Whichever.

Point is, most of my most embarrassing teenage and college-aged memories include Jason, my brother's best friend who quickly assumed the role of my second, surrogate protective older brother. And of course they would. He with the dark hair and smoldering brown eyes. He with his body that's only grown larger and stronger and more muscled over the years.

I blame the wobbly knees and the skip of my heart and the knot in my stomach his mere presence causes for all of it.

From the small scar that remains on my forehead from the first moment, to the embarrassing *outfit change* my dad insisted on when I was a senior in high school. From the night he held my hair back over a toilet when I visited Sawyer in college one weekend while I tried to mutter *Oh my God I love you,* but it came out sounding more like *Oh my Gah blugh blugh blaghck* as I ralphed into a toilet.

Needless to say, our first meeting isn't something a high school girl dreams of when meeting the hottest guy on Earth.

It isn't something forgotten over time when said hottie has the manners to never, ever, ever, bring it up again.

It's simply forgotten.

Hell, it's been so long he probably has forgotten.

I'm the only fool who remembers.

And I hate him for all of it. For his chivalry and his rakish, chiseled looks, and the happy smile he gives to everyone else but me. I hate him for his gorgeous brown eyes and the stupid little bend in his nose and the width of his chest. I hate him for his kindness and the way he's so polite to me.

It completely sucks.

Jason Taylor is not only the hottest guy on Earth... he's quite possibly the nicest. He's also always seen me at my worst when I've always wanted him to see my best.

It's humiliating.

Which is why, walking into Jason's younger brother's back yard patio for a Labor Day party, fully aware most of the team knows of what happened, my eyes are skip, skip, skipping and hopping over every male in attendance. It doesn't take much time before I sense his presence. I've had over a decade to hone my *Jason Taylor is near* alert system. I can sniff him out like a bomb squad dog in an airport.

And for real, people. By executive order of all women everywhere, Jason should have to walk around holding a warning sign. WARNING: MAY MAKE PANTIES WET. PROCEED WITH CAUTION.

It's even worse seeing him in his swim trunks with a

plain white, skintight T-shirt, sauntering toward us. His dark hair swooped to the side, the scruff of his unshaven beard hiding his high cheekbones but somehow illuminating the strength of his jaw.

Jason immediately heads in our direction and I turn my focus to where Sawyer is directing me to an outdoor tiki bar. Music is popping. The sun is shining and the heat is out of this world. Laughter rings out and as we slide through the families, I stop and say hello to the women and players I already know before the man who recently starred in the best *sex dream ever* makes his appearance in front of us, looking so movie-star, ruggedly handsome beautiful I'd be absolutely blinded by him if I wasn't wearing my darkest sunglasses.

"Hey Tessa." He sips a drink out of a red plastic cup, and I instantly want to turn away. His eyes are filled with pity and it's the last thing I want to see when Jason looks at me.

"Be nice today, okay?" Sawyer says and he wiggles his finger between both of us. "I need to grab Debbie something to drink."

I glare at Sawyer's back as he scoots away from us before turning back. "Hey Jason."

"You doing okay?"

"Peachy." It feels like everyone's staring, but a quick look tells me the opposite. No one cares about me or my problems. I'm almost not sure what's worse. "How many know?"

"He called you at practice yesterday, so my guess is..." He shrugs, grins like this doesn't matter. Like the most humiliating day of my life is one big joke. Joke's on him because it totally is a big joke and so am I. "Everyone. Listen, he and I talked, and if you need something, you know I'm here, right? I'm always here to help, with whatever you need."

"I'll be fine."

"But you don't have to be fine alone, either." His jaw hardens. I'm pretty sure his chest puffs up too but I refuse to look below his chin. Sometimes it makes me dizzy.

I know my stubbornness irritates him but I'm not trying to be stubborn. I'm trying to be safe. Between that stupid dream the other night and my lingering questions about the last time I saw him, I don't have a firm handle on how to be around Jason right now. Not when everything else around me is falling apart.

"Fine, then. Thanks for the offer. But really, I'll be fine. I'll figure everything out and move on. So now, if you'll excuse me, I hear there's a baby I have to meet."

I hate I feel this way around him after so many long stupid years. I'm unsettled and rattled and at the end of my rope and the person I should not want to cling to for help above anyone else is Jason Taylor.

Lord knows he'll probably help only because it's ingrained in his DNA to be Mr. Nice Guy. I'm pretty sure if I peel off the white shirt clinging to his skin he'd have a Superman logo stamped on his chest.

I pause in my pursuit of finding Mikah Lutzgo's new baby Debbie gushed over yesterday and head to the bar. I grab a spiked lemonade from a metal tin filled with ice and drinks when I risk a look back at Jason.

He has his head to the sky, corded throat tight and veins popping. Fingers digging into the swim trunks slung low on his hips.

So pretty. So very, very pretty from a distance.

So much more dangerous to my fragile heart at close range.

CHAPTER FIVE

JASON

SAWYER'S GIVEN me shit for years for not settling down. Too bad I can't tell him why. Not that I haven't wanted to.

"Well, gee, mate, see... several years ago, I started realizing how hot your sister is. Then I started realizing how incredibly awesome she is to be around. And then I started realizing how much I really actually liked her. And all these years later, I still can't stop thinking about her."

She might live over seven hundred fifty miles away, but she still has a grip on my dick. I've Google mapped the span of her reach. That's how pathetic I am.

For once I want to finally force her to see what's been in front of her all along. She was eighteen and I was twenty-two the first time I really realized I was starting to like her. I'm pretty sure it came in an overprotective—okay, perhaps slightly jealous moment—when she was getting dressed to go out on a date. I had gotten a glimpse of what she was wearing and my head almost exploded so me, being the dick

I am, I went and gave Mr. Chauncy a heads up so when she came prancing down the stairs on her way out the door, it was *his* head that almost exploded when he saw her in the tight, short black leather miniskirt.

But there was nothing I could do about it then.

We were young, I was just starting my professional playing career. She was in school in an entirely different country. I saw her only a handful of times during that time period. Unfortunately, every time I did see her, she kept getting more and more beautiful. I eventually slowed my trips back to Sawyer's. I made so many excuses he finally confronted me about why I wouldn't go back to Canada with him when before, I went every time he asked.

So, whatever. His sister was hot. My dick wanted her. Tough freakin' life. Puck bunnies at home and on the road became my go-to so I didn't go crazy. Am I proud of it? No. I'm not ashamed either. I treat the women I'm with, with respect and they haven't all been one-night stands. I've casually dated, but there's been two problems keeping me from ever taking things more serious.

One: I didn't like anyone enough to make the effort during the season when we were traveling all the time, and

Two: The blonde beauty in front of me who still makes my dick hard on sight like I haven't grown past that twenty-two-year-old idiot.

With Tessa in town, I have a limited time to set a few things straight, and I don't care what I have to do to get her to listen, but it's happening.

I had every intention of walking up to Tessa this afternoon, flinging out the same shit we always do and yet when I saw her, looking so damn sexy and so damn sad... I couldn't.

In all the years I've been able to push aside my obsession with her which has been absolutely nothing brotherly, that all changed on New Year's. The first, and only time, I've even attempted to approach her with how I feel.

It was the last time I saw her at Hendrix's place with the whole team and she was there, sans Will, whose face I will happily rearrange myself someday. And fuck... I almost kissed her then. In the hallway where it was dark and we delivered our quiet, typical barbs and yet that same electric pulse of attraction was so damn bright and intense I could see everything. Like the way her lashes fluttered at the top of her cheekbones when I leaned in.

It took laughter and one of our defenseman, Duke Fletcher, stumbling drunkenly down the hall, bouncing off walls to regain my wits. This was Tessa, and her brother was fifteen feet away. And oh yeah... at the time, she was engaged. Which meant she wasn't mine to have or tease or flirt with. It doesn't matter that I'd already heard from Debbie and Sawyer things weren't good between them and she was already questioning breaking things off.

Still, she wasn't single or available and I wasn't that kind of asshole. Ever. That night... that night was the first night I was ashamed of my attraction to her because it almost turned me into someone I never wanted to be. The kind of guy who would kiss another man's woman.

Jesus. I scrub a hand down my face, unable to peel my gaze off her as she grabs a drink and turns toward the women who are all in a tizzy over the baby, Hannah, our goalie and Captain Byron Maddox's, wife, is holding. Mikah's. Which is a crazy enough story in itself.

Like always though, it's Tessa who grabs my attention as she stands to the side, jaw falling open as I'm sure someone tells her the story.

Yes! He was abandoned on Mikah's doorstep!

I'm probably imagining the way she smiles, glances at me before looking quickly back to the baby in Hannah's arms. If anyone's lucky, they'll get to hold him at some point but I wouldn't be surprised if Hannah hogs him all day long.

But if Tessa is only here for a few more days, then we need to talk. There're things I have to say.

The last thing I want is for her to head back to Toronto not knowing when I'll see her again and still not have her at least know my true feelings for her.

CHAPTER SIX

Tessa

I'M over this party and this weekend and my stupid life where I've lost everything. I always love coming down to Charlotte to see my brother and Debbie. I love the team. I love the family atmosphere. I know not every hockey team in the country has the family-type bonds they've managed to create here, so these guys are pretty damn lucky. When I'm down here, I get to forget about anything bothering me at home.

But today? It's shaken me in a way I'm not expecting. Debbie is pregnant and shockingly doing a good job of hiding it. I'm pretty sure she's spent the last week trying to recreate her tipsy, drunk laugh because it is *on point* today. And then there's Mikah, the quiet, young player from Denmark who apparently has had his world rocked with a baby being delivered to his doorstep and his new... girlfriend? Paisley? She can barely keep her eyes off him.

Everyone is happy.

Of course they are. This is, after all, a family party where everyone is excited and getting ramped up for the season that starts soon. And me? I'm the twit who dated the loser who stole everything from her and next weekend I get to return to an empty apartment and then my job designing marketing brochures for the bank that brought us together. Where I get to tell all the coworkers we used to be friends with before Will was fired all the awesome things he's done.

Yippee.

Setting down my drink, the only one I've had all day because I'm *not in the mood,* I grab my phone and head back into Jude's house. Maybe a few minutes to close my eyes, breathe deep and reset my attitude will help me get through this until Sawyer and Deb are ready to head home.

Probably where I'll get to listen to them go at it all night.

God. I'm sounding pathetic and I hate I can't shake this off. So I have a failed relationship. So I need to buy new furniture. It's not like I won't be able to find Will and try to have him arrested. That's the first thing I should do. Probably should have done it before I left Toronto but I was too pissed to think straight.

I pull up my reminder app on my phone, set an alert to call the local station first thing in the morning to make a report. They'll take care of the rest. I'm sure of it.

A tiny sliver of hope plants itself in my chest and I inhale a deep breath.

There's a movie room somewhere in this house and I'm hoping it will be dark and that the leather seats will cool down my heated skin from the hours of sunshine.

I wander down the hallway passed a library where kids' laughter and shrieks bounce off the walls with excitement until I find the room I was looking for.

Yes. It's dark and quiet. Exactly what I need. A quick

look down the hall tells me I've gone unnoticed, exactly what I was hoping for when I slunk out of the patio. Inside the dark room, keeping the lights off. The leather cinema-type recliner chairs are black, along with the walls. The only thing of color is the enormous projector screen hanging on the wall. I find a spot in a dark corner, far from the doorway in the last of the sixteen chairs and collapse into it, pulling my feet up onto the chair, knees bent, and press my forehead to them.

The room must be well insulated because I can't hear a thing from outside or down the hall and before I fall asleep in this dark, depressing corner that completely fits my mood, I pull up a meditation app on my phone. Usually I use it when I need to focus. Sometimes to reenergize, but right now I want to settle my mind from everything.

My job. Will. The work ahead for me once I return home. Sawyer and Debbie. Their baby. Possible engagement. And the loudest noise bouncing in my brain, digging claws into my memory banks... Jason.

Stupid, nice, hot guy Jason.

"Ugh." I press my head back into the theatre-style chair, hit the start button on the app and turn down the volume so I have to really concentrate on the voice coming from my phone.

As the app starts, I settle in and get comfortable and listen to the soothing voice guiding me along. I'm relaxed, focusing on the words being spoken and not the thoughts racing in my mind when a shift occurs in the room.

It's Jason, ruining all of my calming progress. I can tell without seeing him. My Taylor-radar never fails. It's somehow connected from the scent of his cologne to the apex of my thighs.

I peel open one eye and *yup*. There he is, in that

skintight white T-shirt and swim trunks, standing in the doorway, one shoulder propped against it.

"Go away," I murmur barely loud enough for him to hear and close my eyes. He won't listen. I know he won't, but I'm still irritated he doesn't.

"I thought you were sleeping."

"I'm not. Taking a break from happy people is all." I can no longer focus on the voice of the app and instead, every nerve ending in my stupid body is alit with glee because *yay! Jason's here!*

Ugh. I need to find a surgeon. One willing to dig into my brain and find all memory traces of Jason in my hippocampus and dig them out. I'm certain at this point in my life it's the only way I'll stop feeling so freaking *giddy* in his presence, despite never wanting to show it.

Who cares if I become mindless afterward. Sawyer would find me the best long-term facility where I can suck down pudding and Jell-O cups all day long.

I ignore Jason as long as possible until the seat next to me creaks and the air heats by several degrees. I'm pretty sure his hotness radiates out from him with a three meter span of constant warmth.

"Will's always been a dick," Jason says and I snort.

"You never liked him even when he was a good guy."

"I'd never like any guy you introduce me to."

Of course he wouldn't. He's taken his big brother role seriously from the moment I clenched his hand in a room at the Urgent Care while a needle shot numbing medication into my scalp. I open my eyes into slits. He's blurry in my narrowed vision and in the dark, it takes me a minute to zone in on him.

"What do you want?"

"I came to see if you were really okay. Saw you outside and you looked pretty miserable."

See? Nicest guy ever. It's too bad he'll never be *my* nice guy. And his presence and kindness is putting a serious kink into my "Get over my stupid crush" plan.

"That's nice of you and all, but I already have one brother looking out for me, I don't really want another right now."

"I'm not your brother."

Yeah. Trust me. I know that very well. I shrug my shoulders and shift in my chair. Perhaps if I start ignoring him, he'll go away and yet I hate the sting in my eyes when I do so, knowing it's because I can't have him. "You know what I mean. I just need a few minutes to chill and then I'll be back out there, okay?"

"I know what you mean, Tessa. But trust me, I've never once thought of myself as your brother."

"What?" My head jerks in his direction and this time, my eyes are wide open.

"You heard me. How drunk were you on New Year's?"

Oh God. My heart is thumping out of control and there's some strange tingle racing down my legs. If I were standing, I'd definitely collapse. I haven't even been quite sure that moment we had was real.

It was?

"New Year's?" I'm almost laughing hysterically at this point.

And yet, he's moving. Closer. Like in slow motion giving me plenty of time to leap and lunge over the rows of chairs to escape and yet somehow, my feet are super glued to the carpet.

I'm too stunned by *all of this because what in the heck!?* I'm stuck here, rooted to my spot while he leans in... so close. So close I can smell his cologne or body wash or maybe it's his natural pheromones that makes him smell so edible. Like candy. Strawberries dipped in chocolate. Sinfully yummy chocolate.

"I wasn't drunk on New Year's." That's right, brain. You can work. Think. Speak. All the good things.

Jason moves closer, looms over me with his brawn and beefy goodness until his lips are at my cheek. I shiver, darn my stupid teenage crush that's only multiplied over the years. I cling to the chair behind me. Otherwise, I'll rip off his shirt, climb him like a tree, and have my way with him and YIKES! *Not good! Abort! Abort!*

"So you remember what I said."

"Umm." I mean, I have this fuzzy memory of him almost kissing me, but surely that can't be what he's implying. Perhaps it was when he asked me if I wanted champagne. Some totally innocuous earlier conversation before the hallway incident.

"Jason." I say nothing else. There isn't anything else to say. "Why did you come in here?"

"Because you're not with Will, and I'm pretty sure that night I gave you a hint of what I was feeling and you froze up. But in case you need it said more clearly, here it is. You're not with Will. And I'm tired of waiting."

Don't ask! Don't ask! Don't even think of asking! "Waiting for what?"

I said don't ask! My brain screams at me. I definitely need to find some mental help pronto.

"You know…" he drawls and it's so irritating how calm he can be right now. "I think I'm going to let you finally figure that out for yourself," he whispers and gah! Why is he doing this and what is this madness. I'm dreaming. I have to be! I pinch myself and squeak from the pain.

He chuckles at my ridiculousness.

He steps back and grins. I can't decide if I want to slap him or kiss him. It's not possible he's meant any of this. No way.

No how.

"Sawyer," I say and I want to slam my hands over my mouth.

Jason's smile falters for only a moment and he shrugs. "Maybe I don't really give a crap of your brother's opinion about what this would be anymore."

What this would be? What would WHAT be? What does he mean!?

He turns then and walks away. He's leaving? After tossing me a grenade with the pin pulled? What do I do with this?

When he gets to the doorway he turns, and I brace myself for the punch line of his joke. *Oh hey, just kidding, Tessa. You're my totally too cute and too young sister. I'm totally messing with you.*

Oh Jason... you funny, funny boy, you.

"I'm going to head home. Want a ride?"

Yeah, I want a ride. Probably not the kind he's thinking of with four wheels in an enclosed vehicle. Mine is more sweaty. Without clothes. On a soft surface. Heck, any surface will do.

"No," I choke out. Bad idea! I'm full of them today! I blame the sun and this wretched heat. Us Canadians aren't equipped to handle it. "No."

"See you soon, then."

The last thing I see is a flash of his sparkling white teeth. I drop back to my chair and somehow, sit right on my phone because beneath my ass a muffled voice says, "Breathe deep."

"Yeah, meditator… I'm breathing deep. Trust me."

"THIS SUCKS." I pop a grape into my mouth and hug the fruit bowl tighter. Apparently fruit is Debbie's first craving and the fridge is stocked with all kinds of it.

"What do you think you'll do?" She's lounging on her couch, feet tucked beneath a blanket. She has dark circles under her eyes and a rumpled tank top on. She came out of the bathroom thirty minutes ago after another morning puke-a-thon, collapsed onto the couch with a pathetic sound, and hasn't moved in hours.

She listened to me call the police department closest to my neighborhood. I was transferred to three different people before finally explaining to a detective what happened last Friday. Unfortunately, everything I learned isn't the greatest news and not much different from what I was expecting. It was our joint bank account. Both of our names are on the apartment lease. All the furniture was purchased from said joint account making it all *ours*. Sure, Will-the-slimeball shouldn't have taken everything and he definitely stole since all the money going into the account was my money.

But as far as recourse? The detective said things could get "sticky." He assured me they'd have officers swing by the apartment and check it out, file a claim. I've called my landlord to ensure the company gives them access considering I'm out of the country. Detective Richard Struble also kindly explained they can enlist the divisions to assist in finding Will if I can send them a recent picture as well as if they can find one of him on a camera, but in all honesty, his lack of enthusiasm doesn't give me much confidence anything will be found. Or if it is, that there's really anything we can do to get it back.

When I called the landlord, I also asked if she can give access for the insurance company whenever I call them to file my claim. Even then, if it's discovered Will took everything, they might not be able to provide any assistance.

In short, none of it looks promising. Even if they find Will, it'll be complicated to prove he stole from me. All the bank records show are withdrawals made starting a week ago which I never caught.

"I don't know what I'll do." I toss another grape into my mouth and chew slowly.

"You can stay here," Debbie says and I laugh quietly.

"Right. I'll just move on in." Don't get me wrong, their place is really nice. They live in a decent-sized townhouse, and while I know it's expensive due to its location in a ritzy area of Charlotte, the home isn't that large. I can stand at the kitchen island and overlook the entire downstairs. The kitchen opens up to the dining area and the living room behind it. It's gorgeous and updated with gleaming white woodwork and sparkling wood floors and a wood stairway that leads to the bedrooms upstairs. But it's only two bedrooms. And as I've recently learned, built with thin walls.

I used to tease Sawyer about his humble home considering the money he made but stopped the day he turned to me and replied, "I can live like a king for a short time, or ensure I live easy forever." Sawyer's always claimed he knows his professional career won't last forever and while he's one of the highest-paid defenseman in the league, he's still thirty-three years old. He doesn't have many years left if he keeps being hard on his body. I know when he retires, he wants to be able to maintain his standard of living while never having to worry about money. Now that his family is expanding, I can't imagine they'll stay here. He'll want a yard for his child to run in someday, maybe a pool.

"It doesn't have to be permanent. But you have more vacation time, right? You can stay until your next paycheck comes and the insurance claim goes through. At least then you don't have to sleep on your floor and live on ramen."

"I like ramen."

"You're also stubborn."

"It's a Chauncy family trait."

"I'm well aware," she drolls. Reaching over to her bowl of oyster crackers, she tosses one at my face and then plops back to the couch. "God. Every time I move I think I'm going to puke."

"You shouldn't have let my brother put his woohoo in you then."

She waggles her brows and smirks. "Your brother's woohoo—"

"Enough!" I slam my hands over my ears. I started this, but that's enough. I should have known better than to have said anything. The thought of Sawyer's willy or woohoo or whatchamacallit getting anywhere near Debbie makes *me* be the one who's going to vomit.

Her laugh is sweet but short, quickly followed by a moan. "You're supposed to head back in a few days and on top of working you have to deal with all this bologna. Why don't you stay here a couple more weeks?"

I can call my boss. Email him. Antoine Benoit is a really decent man and a great boss. If I tell him Will took all my belongings, he'll probably set me up in his family's guest bedroom. Sharing a house with four kids under the age of eight isn't really my idea of a great time.

"I don't know..."

Maybe I don't really give a crap of your brother's opinion about what this would be anymore. It's not the first or the thousandth time Jason's words have slithered through my mind since yesterday. I lost my train of thought so much earlier talking to Detective Stroble I'm pretty certain he thinks I'm making this whole thing up. Surely people who are telling the truth can say it much more effectively than the constant stammers of "uhs" and "huhs" I used.

But it's Jason. The very last thing I was expecting was for him to say that and I'm still not sure I heard him correctly. I mean, why? Why now? And what does it really mean?

I think I should call his team doctor, maybe have *his* head examined for all the strange things he said to me the other day at that pool party. *He* wanted to talk to me? Take care of me? Now in addition to having to figure out my life in Canada, I have to figure out what in the world to do with the dark-haired—and most likely concussed—man I've always loved.

The hits just keep on coming and one more might knock me out completely.

"It could be great though, if you want to stay longer. You can help me start picking things out for the baby. Or decorate the nursery. And... if you decide you like it here, then you can see your little niece or nephew grow up. Wouldn't that be wonderful?"

Debbie's usually pretty perky. She was a natural-born and good cheerleader all through high school. What she's not usually is manipulative.

My eyes narrow. "Did Sawyer try to convince you into talking me into this?"

He's been at the training facility all day.

She has the grace to blush, but her hand slips to her still

completely flat stomach and rubs gentle circles. "No. Why ever would you think that?"

I snort and stab a piece of melon with a fork. "I'll think about it."

After all, what exactly is waiting for me back home?

CHAPTER SEVEN

JASON

"WELL GET me somcone who does not cry all the time then."

I can't help but laugh at the way Sylvia, our team's travel director, barks through the phone. She's a robust Russian woman, almost my mother's age. She's as terrifying as facing down Washington's enforcer who's given me more than a few black eyes over the years. On the inside, I'm convinced she's sweet as apple pie. I enjoy trying to dig that part out of her.

Pretty sure she likes to pretend she hates me for it.

I'm outside her office today only because I need to let her know my parents won't be coming to watch our pre-season games this year. They tend to alternate trips between seeing Jude and I play and our little brother Joey out in Las Vegas. This year, it was their turn for our pre-season where they were supposed to spend a few nights in hotels and join us on the road. The guys love it when my dad is with us.

Coaches too. Yeah, my dad's a legend, but he's also damn fun and slightly crazy. But since Jude was injured last season, they want to make sure they're here for our first home game stretch instead.

Enter Sylvia.

As the team's travel director, she's essentially our boss when we travel. She takes care of the entire team and coaches' schedules, ensuring we all have rooms and room-mates we don't hate. She makes sure busses are scheduled to take us from hotels to arenas. That we eat on time. That our gear doesn't get lost. She's our mom. A mean one. I'm pretty sure she wishes she could paddle us with our sticks when we don't listen to her.

Listening to her shout into her phone over another lost assistant? Hilarious. It's a demanding job during the season and I have a lot of respect for the members of our team who don't take to the ice but take care of all of us in the back-ground. But Sylvia goes through assistants faster than I go through stick tape.

Wait. Hold up a second....

She's still shouting as the thought forms. I should prob-ably call Sawyer. Have him float this idea out. But nope, this is it... my opportunity.

I knock on Sylvia's door while she continues ranting in her thick Russian accent about not needing pansy assistants who can't do their jobs. She either doesn't hear it or ignores me, but I enter despite the risks of her throwing a flaming dart at my chest.

She glares at me and slams her phone down. "Vhat do you vant?" It's amazing after all this time in the States, at least thirty years, her W's still sound like V's.

"Maybe if you stopped making them all cry, someone

would stick around." I think Sylvia's turnover ratio on assistants is higher than the team's trading average.

She gives me a look that can kill a hard-on. "You are bugging me. And I am busy."

"I have someone—"

Her glare narrows. Pretty sure she's at risk of snapping the pen in her hand and it looks metal.

"You know. On second thought, never mind. She's probably too nice to work for you."

I don't need to help out Tessa, convince her to take this job and maybe move here only to have Sylvia kill her soul.

"Not interested in one of your floozies—"

"It's Chauncy's sister. And who in the hell still says floozies?"

She taps her pen to the desk, lips pressed into a pout. When Sylvia frowns, a grouping of lines burrow deep into her forehead.

"Humph," she finally grunts. "I can try to be nice to her. For Sawyer. He's a nice boy."

I'm pretty sure Sawyer hasn't been called a boy since he was nine.

"But not me?" I press my hand to my chest and give her a puppy dog look. I swear the woman loves me. Deep down, deep, deep down in her tiny black heart. "Sylvia. I'm hurt."

"To be hurt you'd have to have heart." Takes one to no one, I suppose. "Have her email me her resume or call me if she's interested." She flips her hand in the air. "Now go. You bug me too much."

In my mind I hear it as *Jason Taylor, you are my favorite boy on the team. Come on in and kick your feet up. Stay awhile.*

"I actually did come up here with something else to tell you." I push off the wall of her office and duck as the pen she's holding flies at my head. "Hey! No stabbing the assistant captain! Coach has already warned you about this."

I grin as I bend down and pick it up.

"Vhat do you vant."

I take a slow, cautious step toward her desk and set down the pen. "My parents' schedule has changed. But—" I lift my hands in the air before she throws something else at me. "This makes it easier for you. No traveling. They'll only be here for the home games and they're staying with Jude."

And Lord help him and Katie for it.

She scribbles something down on a notepad in front of her and doesn't look at me. "Any work more than what I had is not easy. Spoiled boys. All of you. What else?"

"Nothing, except I'd love to say that the color of your shirt makes you look very beautiful today."

She's wearing a black shirt. She always wears a black shirt. And in all honesty, it makes her look a little washed out, but I love my balls way too much to ever say such a thing.

I grin shamelessly. I have two goals in life. Get Tessa to admit she loves me and get Sylvia here to admit she doesn't want me to die in a fiery inferno.

"Humph." She goes back to writing my death plans but I swear I see a smile. Just a twitch.

I wait until after Sawyer and I are done working out in the team's training facility before I approach Sawyer about my idea. Mostly it's because I want to be the one to bring it up with Tessa.

She'll probably growl at me for getting involved in her life, tell me how stupid I am for thinking this. Hell, she does have a job and a life in Canada and even without dipshit Will who will lose his balls someday soon, she has to have friends. A social life. Co-workers. Maybe she doesn't *want* to consider something else.

Which is why it's important I see her face to face when I bring this up because I know Tessa better than I know how to read the puck on the ice.

I'm spotting Sawyer as he bench presses, biting my tongue with my excitement over this opportunity. Hell, he loves Tessa. He'll probably champion it before he considers what it means to work for Sylvia. I don't doubt he'd love to have her close. Their parents, while incredible, are also pretty anti-social and homebodies. They're sweet people, full of open arms and refrigerators for when I'd come to visit but I know they prefer to stick close to their small town forty-five minutes outside Toronto. They rarely watch Sawyer play anymore because they don't like to fly and other than their annual cruise they take over New Year's, the only games I've seen them at are when we're within driving distance.

Which means while Tessa might have friends in Toronto, she doesn't have a lot of family.

She'd have so much more if she considered this.

"You and Debbie have any plans tonight?" I try for casual but I'm not sure it comes out right based on the look he gives me.

"On a Tuesday? Not real wild plans, no."

"Want company? Figure I can bring dinner from that Indian place you both like so much." Bonus, Tessa loves their butter chicken.

I mostly enjoy the way she eats her food with naan, slurping it off her fingers. It's given me a few boners over the years.

Sawyer's brows pull together and he grunts, lifting the

weight bar over his face before settling it into the rack. "What are you doing?"

"Nothing."

"Right." He sits and presses a towel to his face. "You haven't offered to deliver food to Debbie and me since... wait..." He snaps his fingers and smirks. "You've *never* offered to bring us food. This about Tessa?"

It's possible she has something to do with it. After I left the movie room yesterday, I spent most of the day feeling like a total jerk. She's going through enough right now without having someone pressure her. Which is why I stepped back and left when all I wanted to do was lean in and stay. Forever. At least long enough to slide my mouth against hers and kiss her like I really want to.

But pushing her while she's reeling from all of Will's bullshit won't help anything right now. Especially not with this new plan. I need to slow down and be steady. Give her little hints of what I want. What she means to me.

"Can't a guy do something nice for his friends?" He gives me a look that says plenty. "Fine. I have something I want to talk to her about. Figured it'd be better if everyone was there."

Sawyer huffs and lays back down. "I don't know why in the hell you two can't get along. Two of my most favorite people and you're always at each other's throats." He grumbles it more to himself and since I can't argue, I stay silent.

It's my typical M.O. when it comes to his questioning of Tessa and me.

"But yeah." He grunts and lifts the weight bar again. "You want to bring me food, I won't turn you down. Want to tell me what it is you're thinking of for Tessa?"

"I think it'll be more fun as a surprise."

"Great." He chuckles. "She loves those."

She hates them. I can't blame her. I don't like them either, mostly because they're like presents from your grandmother. Someone blows something up, makes it seem like it's *so awesome and the best thing ever* and then you're left forcing a smile because it's absolutely nothing close to anything you wanted.

"Yeah. Not sure she'll like this one either, but you and Debbie will."

He pauses mid-lift. "What in the hell are you talking about?"

"You'll see. You're the only one I know who likes surprises."

"And Debbie."

Debbie hates them. She humors them for Sawyer's sake because he's like a little kid who barely got away with stealing his grandma's chocolate stash.

"All right. And Debbie."

"What? She does."

"I agreed with you."

"You don't sound like you mean it." He shoves the weight bar back into position and sits again. "Does she not like them?"

His face pales, which is weird considering he's sweating buckets.

"Why? What are you planning?"

"Nothing." He wipes off his face and then groans. "Fuck. I have... I have this whole thing planned... and if she'll hate it..."

"What are you talking 'bout?"

"Proposing," he says and the word is almost choked out.

"Are you serious?"

"Yeah. Yeah I am." He's paling more now and for a

moment I want to give my friend shit but he looks utterly terrified. "Yeah. I want to ask her to marry me."

"Well, shit, Sawyer. That's fucking awesome!"

"She hasn't said yes yet."

I slap his shoulder as he stands and we switch positions. "She will. She wouldn't have put up with your lazy ass for this long if she wasn't in it for the long haul."

Something else flashes across his face. More fear than humor and as I settle onto the bench, I punch him lightly in the gut. "You okay? You're not really worried, are you?"

As far as I know, there's no way Debbie will say no. They've been together for years already. Hell, she's probably wondering why it hasn't happened yet.

"No. Nah, man. I'm not worried. I've got this."

"Damn straight."

CHAPTER EIGHT

Tessa

THERE ARE few things I love in life more than my family and running on a brisk fall morning where the air chills your lungs and the scent of dry leaves is heavy in the air.

One of them being Indian food.

Which is why it's currently, almost impossible for me to have any scathing or sarcastic comment at the ready when my brother says we're not cooking dinner tonight because Jason is bringing dinner from Tandor's Kitchen.

Only the best, and my most favorite place, to grab butter chicken when I'm in Charlotte. A fact Jason knows so while I'm on guard when he enters my brother's front door, the smell of my dinner keeps me from asking what this new game is.

Unfortunately, as soon as the aroma hits Debbie, she slams her hand to her mouth and takes off running up the stairs, shouting out a "be back in a sec!" to the rest of us.

"What's going on with her?" Jason asks, hands still holding plastic takeout bags, having kicked off his sandals.

Sawyer took off after Debbie, which means I have to answer.

"Don't know." I shrug and head toward my dinner. "Is this a typical thing, you bringing my brother and his girl-friend dinner?"

"As Sawyer reminded me earlier, it's something I've never done before."

Hmmm. He definitely has something up his sleeves. Sleeves, by the way, that are currently bulging around his biceps in his short sleeve simple gray shirt. I reach for one of the bags but he swings them out of my way, lifting those veined and muscled arms over my head and heads toward the kitchen.

"Easy, killer. You'll get your food if you act like a good little girl."

Being patronized shouldn't send a shiver of excitement down my spine. It's probably the chicken. I fantasize about food from Tandor's almost as frequently as I fantasize about the tight ass in black shorts walking away from me.

Ugh. I want to kick Sawyer in the shin for taking off after Debbie. Damn him and his concern for his pregnant girlfriend. Please. Women have been doing this since the beginning of time. She's *fine*. It's me who currently needs the help. Help not shoving my hands to Jason's stomach and running my fingers all over the muscled blocks that make up his abs.

Help in not restarting the conversation he brought up yesterday. Sawyer doesn't need that bomb ticking down in his house over dinner. I imagine Indian foods are messy when they explode.

I follow after Jason, because darn it... I'm *hungry*. A late afternoon run in the heat wore me out but sometimes running is the best way for me to process my emotions and settle my stress. Debbie's offer to stay awhile longer, an extended vacation, actually sounds delightful. I've never gotten to see my brother's training camps and pre-season games before. He usually only flies me down in the winter, when they're focused on making the playoffs, and for a break for me to get away from Toronto's winters.

Ever since I showered off after my run, I've debated emailing my boss and discussing the possibility with him. I even brought my laptop so I can work remotely for a few weeks if he'd prefer. I don't need to sit around all day doing nothing. Especially with Debbie not feeling well. It's not like we can do all the things we usually do: shop, eat, drink, an occasional day trip to Asheville to tour the Biltmore.

Which is a bummer because they currently have an exhibit from the show Downton Abbey I'm *dying* to walk through.

By the time I shake off my thoughts and reach the kitchen, Jason has the takeout containers he brought set all over the kitchen island and the sacks are thrown in the trash. He's helped himself to a bottle of water and has a few more set out as well.

"What's the occasion for dinner if you don't usually do it?" I twist off the top of a bottled water and take a healthy drink. I should probably go grab my personal water bottle I left in the guest room but the stairs right now would be a killer on my thighs. A five-mile run in ninety-degree heat was probably stupid.

Necessary, but stupid.

"Can't I do something nice without having to have a motive?"

Unfortunately, he probably can because he's that nice,

but in this instance? I don't buy it. "From my favorite restaurant?"

"Oh? You like Tandor's?"

His smirk and gleam in his eyes belies the innocence in his tone. Whatever. If I wasn't already so confused and replaying every single thing that happened yesterday, I'd probably be willing to play this game with him.

As it is, I really am starving. Thankfully, the meals are enclosed in plastic bowls with clear tops so I grab a plate, a few pieces of naan and the container holding my meal and take it to the dining table. I will Debbie to get over her quick bout of nausea so I'm not stuck alone with Jason much longer. I've had days to process their news, but I still can't believe it. Sawyer's going to be a dad and I'm going to be the awesomest aunt in existence.

"What's the happy thought for?"

"What?"

"You're smiling. I don't usually see that when you're around me."

"That's because you're not funny." I stick out my tongue like I'm twelve before shoving a chunk of chicken into my mouth. "Nothing. Just happy to spend time with Sawyer, I guess."

But when his baby is born, I won't be here. Which sucks. A lot. Unless I can be here. Which... is possible. Maybe? My mind has to stop this constant merry-go-round. Go home or stay? It's giving me vertigo.

"Right." His lips press down and I know he doesn't believe me, but Jason seems pretty clueless about Debbie's runoff earlier which tells me the team still doesn't know.

Like he knows the direction of my thoughts, he tilts his head and points his own fork toward the stairway. "She okay? Sawyer didn't say she was sick."

"Dunno." I scoop more chicken onto a folded chunk of naan and moan as I savor the taste. There are some decent restaurants where I live, all within walking distance, which is a bonus, but none are as good as Tandor's. I can't even piece together what makes it so delicious but it's mouth-watering amazing.

"Jesus, Tessa. Can you not sound like you're having an orgasm when you eat?"

I choke on my chicken and wash it down with my water. "Don't like it, you can leave."

"But then I won't be able to share with you why I'm here."

The chicken I've devoured rolls in my stomach. Obviously it's not because he's a nice guy. I lean back in my chair. "What is it?"

He huffs a laugh and I hate he looks so damn good, smirking at me, shaking his head like I'm some amusing little thing.

"You're cute, Tessa. I ever tell you that?"

"I think the day you took me to get stitches in my head, yeah. You bopped me on the nose with a finger and said *'cute and tough, nice'* before ignoring me the rest of the weekend."

I'm mortified with myself. He's not supposed to know these things, know how much I remember *every.single.encounter* with him ever.

His mouth opens a bit and he stares at me. Yeah. That dose of word vomit probably surprises the hell out of him too. But hell, in for a penny. He says he doesn't give a shit about what Sawyer thinks? He should know what I think.

"I'm pretty sure that's the day I started having a crush on you."

He doesn't take his eyes off me as he chews on what I

think is chicken tikki masala. Slowly, he swallows and sets his own fork down. Leaning forward, elbows on the table, I'm tempted to drop my gaze to his mouth and watch his full lips move so sexily as he opens his mouth and asks, "Want to know when it started for me? When I started facing the reality that it was my best friend's little sister that made my dick hard in my dreams at night and when I was on the road?"

No. No. I absolutely do not want to know this. No one should want to know this. This whole game he's playing is ridiculously stupid and a waste of time.

"Jason—"

"Christmas time your junior year. You were headed out with some boyfriend and you were wearing a skintight white sweater that showed off your chest and a black leather skirt so short your dad made you go change it. And it wasn't the skirt that made me hard, it was that you did it, rolling your eyes knowing you wouldn't be able to go out with something so short, but it was the jeans you had on when you came back down. They cupped your ass so damn perfectly I actually jerked off to you that night and you were only sleeping a few feet away from me. I spent so much time that night, pissed off you were able to go out with some other guy, hating that I was too old for you, that Sawyer would kick my ass if I ever did make a move, and I wanted to pummel the guy who got to put his hands on you."

My breath lodges in my throat sometime during his story. My fingers are shaking, and that tremble at the tops of my thighs has absolutely nothing to do with my run from earlier.

"What?" is all I can manage to ask. Jason stares me

down like I'm someone suspected of a crime and he's the detective doesn't believe my alibi.

"Want to know something else about that night?"

"Not really." But oh yes, I absolutely want to know *everything*. Tell me more. Tell me more!

He tilts his head and his thick, brown hair flops over one of his ears, curling in a ridiculously cute way. "I saw you when you were getting dressed. And I was the one who told your dad so he'd make you change."

"What?" It takes me a moment to even *remember* that night. But now I do. Vividly. Because I'd borrowed that tight miniskirt from my friend, knowing Jason would be there and hoping he'd see me in it. That was a decade ago. And he's saying that was when he started noticing me? I can't believe this. Not even because I don't want to... my brain is literally incapable of comprehending this.

I say his name on a breath before asking, "Why are you doing this?"

My hands are shaking so bad I shove them between my knees and press them close together. Heat tumbles through me, sparking emotions and why do I feel like *crying* right now? This should make me happy.

Him being so brutally honest should make me want to jump onto the table, throw our food to the floor and slam my mouth to his, dig my fingers into his hair and kiss the hell out of him. Tandor's be damned! This is what I've always wanted!

Instead, all I want to do is run out the door and all the way back to Toronto.

"I told you. I'm tired of waiting."

CHAPTER NINE

JASON

IT'S possible I should have finessed this a bit more. Tessa gives me absolutely no reaction except calmly pushing back from the table and looking at whatever is suddenly so fascinating behind me.

"I'm going to go check on Debbie and Sawyer."

She turns, heads to the stairs and disappears up them without a backward glance.

"What the hell?" I mutter once she's gone.

I mean, I expected a reaction. That's what Tessa does. I push buttons. She shoves back. It's not even the first time I've hinted at how much I still want her. New Year's Eve comes to mind but that's mostly because I was celebrating the return of my brother to town even if he still couldn't play. I drank too much whiskey and before I was thinking, I for one, swung Katie through the air, giving him shit about her really wanting me and then I caught a glimpse of Tessa, her blonde hair, her sparkling eyes as she laughed easily with Debbie and Regan and a few other wives.

I'd waited for her. Almost took what wasn't mine to have... but now it *could* be, and at the first possible chance, I've stunned Tessa so much she doesn't have a single comeback for me.

It's never happened. We trade barbs. We sling insults. Perhaps it's possible that while we've been at each other's throats over the years, we've never once spilled truths.

She's not gone long though because as her feet are still pounding up the wood stairs, others echo as well and together, both she and Sawyer come back down the stairs. Sawyer, looking a little green in the face and Tessa looking like she's being walked to her public execution.

"What's going on?" It's Sawyer's face that has me pushing back my chair with such force it falls to the floor. "Debbie okay?"

"Yeah, man, she'll be fine." He scrubs a hand down his face and his head falls forward. "I only have a couple more weeks of watching her go through this shit all damn day. I'm over it."

"What are you talking about?"

"She's pregnant, dumbass," Tessa says, grinning at me. Aaah. The name-calling. Apparently she was able to realign our fighting positions on her short run from me.

Silly girl. If I can chase a puck flying a hundred miles across the ice she has to know I can chase—and catch —her too.

"Debbie's pregnant?" Slowly, her words click in my brain. Followed by Sawyer's announcement earlier. "Is this why you want to propose?"

"Well, yeah. And no. I mean, no shit, I don't want to

propose because she's pregnant, but yeah, I want to marry her."

He shakes his head like he needs to clear it and heads toward the island. "She's been sick. Morning. Afternoons. Smells set her off. Sometimes something sounds good and I go pick it up for her and then she throws up as soon as she sees it. This pregnancy shit sucks so far."

"Poor you," Tessa says, patting him on his shoulder. "You're suffering *so* much."

"Shut up." He kicks the back of her butt. "I don't like seeing Debbie like this. It's messing with my head. I mean she's pregnant and we should be happy, but she's miserable. I *made* her miserable, and now I can't fix it."

"Ahhh. I didn't know you had such a soft heart, Chauncy." He glares at me and I'm still baffled at everything. How quickly everything's changing. "How is she now?"

"She wants naan, ginger ale, and to be left alone. Apparently, I'm hovering."

Tessa snickers and quickly loads up a plate of bread and grabs a can of ginger ale from the fridge. "I'll take this up to her then."

She hurries past both of us while keeping her head down. Ahh... still avoiding. No worries though. I don't have anything to do tonight except wait for her to return so I can actually spill why I'm here.

"You tell her your surprise yet?" Sawyer asks. He's digging through the other meals I brought over and loading up a plate.

"Nah, I was waiting for you to hear it too. Figure you might be the one to talk her into it."

"Talk Tessa into something? Have you met her?"

I shake my head and laugh. Yeah, I've met her. "Which is exactly why I might need your help."

"You're right," Tessa says from the living room, coming down the stairs and headed back toward us. She focuses on Sawyer like I'm not standing two feet away from him. "She doesn't even want me to hang out with her. Poor woman."

"All right, then." Sawyer takes his plate to the table, snagging a bottled water on the island on the way. "So now that we're all here together, Jason has something he wants to share with you."

That pulls her to a direct stop. I'm pretty certain she thinks I've shared enough based on the look on her face. Perhaps I should have bit my tongue earlier, laid out the job first and *then* said the rest.

I've never claimed to be the smartest man in the room.

"Ah, yes. The reason for all the free food from my favorite restaurant. Something tells me my butter chicken was meant to butter me up for something else, right?" She slides into her chair at the table like she hasn't been trying to avoid me and places her hands in her lap.

I take the seat across from her. Sawyer's already sitting on her side which is better. Perfect, really. I glance in his direction first. "Sylvia had another assistant quit today."

"What?"

"Pam quit. I overheard Sylvia on the phone with Human Resources needing a new assistant."

"And... oh. Are you serious?" His brows arch into perfect points slowly. I can almost hear pieces clicking together in his brain. For a guy good with handling a stick and defending the goal, he's not the brightest bulb in the box.

"Who's Sylvia?" Tessa asks. Her face is scrunched and I know she's trying to place the name because she's met her before briefly. And anyone who Sawyer and I would talk about would be related to the team.

"Travel director," Sawyer says. "Russian woman, sweet as cherry pie to me and apparently, I think what Jason's trying to say is she has an opening for an assistant."

"And?"

I prop my elbows on the table, hands clasped together and wait for her to give me her attention. "And she said if you're interested, call her or email her your resume."

"No shit?" Sawyer says. His grin splits his face and he laughs. "Damn, Tessa, that'd be awesome! You could travel with us and everything like Sylvia does."

"I have a job," Tessa says and it's possible she's speaking slower, like maybe she thinks I'm an idiot. "In Toronto. In a whole different country."

Seven hundred and fifty miles away. Like I need the reminder.

Sawyer waves her off. "You have dual citizenship and can work here no problem."

I've never been happier she was born outside Buffalo, New York and then moved to Canada as a toddler. I hadn't even considered her citizenship in question when I mentioned her to Sylvia.

I lean forward. "You also have an empty apartment thanks to that dickwad you were smart enough to leave and you have a job for a bank you've always said is *just a job*. I figured maybe if you had the opportunity to do something different, you'd take it."

Bonus to me: Sawyer was right about the traveling. She'd be with me on the road. Err... us. The team. Not *me* me. I'm shocked I haven't actually considered what that would mean before now.

Tessa, tucked away in a hotel room probably to herself

on the road while I'm stuck sharing the room with Jude or Byron. Team learned years ago not to put Sawyer and me together. We don't get any sleep. I could visit her.

My dick jerks at the thought and I grit my teeth to will away any hint of an erection.

She curls her lip at me, eyes narrowed. "Thanks for reminding me how much my life sucks, Jason. Really appreciate it."

"Hey. I'm not trying to do that. I heard Sylvia on the phone this morning when I went to talk to her about changing plans for my parents and I heard she needed help. I thought, maybe... *maybe*... now that you're not tied to Toronto because of Will or anything, you might think it'd be cool to do something different. Maybe you'd want to be close to Sawyer." If her brother isn't enough to get her here because I'm sure as hell not mentioning *me* right now, the news they've just told me has to seal the deal. "Plus, then you can be around when you become an aunt, instead of watching Sawyer and Debbie's baby grow up on FaceTime."

She narrows her eyes at me. Like she hadn't thought of that. No way will she tell me I'm right, though. She doesn't have it in her. She probably won't be brave enough to share her excitement at the thought. Fortunately, Sawyer has no freaking problems.

This is all working out in my favor. I didn't even know about her becoming an aunt when I came up with this idea, but if I know Tessa as well as I think I do... that will definitely be the selling point.

"Oh shit!" Sawyer shouts. "I didn't even think of that! That'd be so awesome." He throws his arms around his sister and yanks her to him. Her head flops onto his shoulder like a rag doll and while she's still trying to scowl at me, her grin is breaking through. "You have to do this! And bonus, you're already packed."

I laugh and immediately school my features when Tessa glares at me. "Thanks, bro."

She jabs her fingers into his ribs and he lets her go. "Hey, I mean, there's a silver lining to Will being a jerk to you after all."

"Right," she snorts. For a while, she doesn't say anything, but she digs back into her dinner even though I'm sure by now it's not even warm. She chews a bite and grimaces. Before she can get up, I grab the container and plop it into the microwave. "So what does a travel director or their assistant do?"

"Sylvia's our Queen on the Road," Sawyer says. I focus on the spinning in the microwave with precision, choosing to ignore her question. I've done my part. Sawyer can manage the rest. Him having a baby is the *best possible thing* though that could have happened today. Certainly makes my hope she stays possible. "She manages all our travel arrangements, deals with families coming on the road. She's the one who schedules flights, plans out equipment arrivals. She kicks our ass if we're late for the bus or plane. I doubt we could survive a road game without her."

"And she travels to *all* the games?"

"Most of them, I think. Playoffs definitely. Usually weekends when we have quick turn-arounds she goes, but for some games, if we're going to one town and then back, she might stay here."

"And who goes?"

"The assistants," I say. The microwave dings and I can't hide the look in my eyes. The thought of having Tessa on the road and not have to rely on my hand? I've mentally jumped ten thousand steps ahead of where we are, but it's where we're going. Once Tessa falls in line with my way of thinking anyway.

I slide her container back in front of her and I'm pretty sure the pink on her cheeks has nothing to do with the steamy heat coming from her meal.

"So... move here, work on your team..." Her mouth opens and shuts. Three times before she frowns. "I can't stay here," she says to Sawyer. "You and Debbie will be planning for a baby and you'll need that room."

"So stay with me," I say. And hot damn, this day is getting better and better. I didn't even imagine *this scenario* eight hours ago. "I have the space, and once the season starts, I'll hardly be there."

"Stay with you?" She points a fork at my face but I catch the slight waver in it.

I lean forward. "Why not? What would be wrong with that?"

In truth, she's never actually admitted to having a crush on me before tonight. But I'm not blind. I've seen the way she blushes. The way when she was younger she stammered over her words around me, or glared daggers at women I was with. Even while she was with Will, I will swear on my grave that she still blushed and got nervous around me. Sometimes I'm certain she fights with me just so she doesn't let her brother know how much she likes me. She's a bit like Sylvia in that, so I suspect they'll get along great. Perhaps I've gotten this all wrong in my head and she doesn't want me. So she had a crush on her brother's older friend years ago. That doesn't mean she still does. Hell, she was engaged.

Perhaps she's moved on.

The thought almost makes me growl, but I swallow it down. It only makes my job harder, but still not impossible.

Sawyer jumps in, saving me from pushing her on this. "Think about it, Tessa. Obviously you can stay here as long as you want, but you'd have more space at Jason's. He has the pool and a gym. That'd be good with all the running you like to do. But it's not like Debbie is going to pop out the kid tomorrow, so you have time to think about what you want to do."

"I might if this *kid* keeps making me throw up." Debbie's in the living room, slowly heading our way, empty plate of food held in one hand and no longer a green hue to her skin. "What'd I miss about Tessa having time to think?"

"Apparently these guys," Tessa says, flicking her fork back and forth between us. "Have decided my future, my job, and my living arrangements and they've done it all without either considering *my* thoughts or desires or remembered I'm even in the same room with them."

Debbie snorts and kisses the top of Tessa's head as she passes, earning her another scowl. "Well, what is it they're planning? Can't be much different than what we talked about earlier."

Nice. I like how this is going. I swallow the bite of food in my mouth and say, "We're trying to convince Tessa to move down here and go to work with Sylvia. She has an opening."

The plate falls from Debbie's hands and she throws her hands in the air. She rushes back to Tessa, yanking her into a hug from behind so she's practically choking Tessa in her seat. "Oh my gosh, Tessa! This is awesome! You have to, you have to!"

Tessa sighs and closes her eyes. When she opens them again, she's shooting fire from them. Aimed directly at me.

I sit back in my chair and smile.

CHAPTER TEN

Tessa

JASON *FREAKING* TAYLOR.

If I could reach him quick enough, I'd stab him with my fork. I cannot *believe* the way this night has gone. Not only has he thrown me onto a roller coaster without a safety bar, it's possible he's ruined the taste of Tandor's Kitchen for me forever.

I'm not sure which I'm more angry about.

His high-handed way to get me close to him—his suggestion to *move in with him* because seriously. Ha. We'll kill each other. Or maybe I'm the only one worried about serving twenty-five to life. He seems pretty pleased with himself as I sit across from him, fuming, Debbie's arms still wrapped around my throat while he re-explains his morning to Debbie.

"This would be so wonderful!"

She's happy. She's felt like crap for weeks and I'm pretty sure this is the first thing that's made her smile. I'm the pin, headed toward a balloon and spoiling a child's birthday.

"As enticing as this is," I say, hissing out the words through clamped teeth, aiming my fire at Jason.

He grins at me like he doesn't notice. "It is enticing, isn't it? All of it..."

I don't know the game he's playing but I do know I didn't sign up for it. The way he's looking at me lets me know exactly what part he finds enticing. The living together part.

And holy crapoly. Living together? What planet has this alien Jason come from? I should call *Ghostbusters*. I'm pretty certain a foreign being invaded his body based on his behavior this last weekend.

"Like I was saying. As cool as that would be, I don't know if that's something I'm prepared to do."

"Why not?" Sawyer sounds like I kicked his puppy. "I mean, it'd be so awesome. Us being close. It's not like you see mom and dad much so that won't change, and wouldn't it be fun to be here? And traveling with your big bro? C'mon...that'd be the best."

It's like Sawyer has still never figured out the only reason I started working in high school was to *avoid* his hockey games. It's not that I don't like the sport. Or that I don't love him. And yeah, I really do love watching him play professionally, but geez... do I want my career to be tied to his?

Debbie squeezes me because out of everyone, she understands.

Across the table, Jason's smile diminishes. Yeah, pretty sure he gets it, too.

"Right," he says. He grabs his own takeout that hasn't

been eaten and heads toward the kitchen. "Think about it, Tessa. I get it, either way."

His voice has mellowed. He's lost the teasing and I don't guess why he seems to suddenly not care at all what I decide one way or the other. He once confessed he worried that his littlest brother Joey only got into hockey because it was expected of him. I mean, the guy now plays professionally too, so maybe Jason was wrong all those years ago, but being the youngest brother to three hockey star brothers and a legacy father couldn't have been easy for him. I've never met him, though, but it's like a switch has been flipped and Jason gets his error.

Yeah, I may not want my life to go back to revolving around Sawyer's career.

But to be honest... the job? How freaking cool. I'd love to travel, see the games from behind the scenes. I'd get to see all parts of the United States and Canada.

It's the whole *Jason and so much time together* part that has my hands shaking. And live with him?

Ha. No freaking way.

"I'll consider it," I finally say and Debbie kisses my cheek.

"Good." I'm not surprised by her reaction considering it's exactly what she proposed earlier today. At least staying for longer. Maybe I do have some time to figure it out, yeah?

"YOU WILL LET me know whichever you choose, yes?"

I grin into the phone. Antoine, my boss, is the best. After two days of coercion, compliments of Sawyer and Debbie trying to convince me to at least apply for the position with the Ice Kings, I've finally decided to call my boss and request an extended vacation. I explained what happened with my belongings and apartment and he let loose a string of both French and English curse words before finally getting a hold of himself.

Then he replied, as easily as I knew he would and said, "You can always stay with us, cherie."

Hahaha. Nope. Definitely not doing that. But staying with Sawyer? If I have to listen to him and Debbie going at it morning and night and her vomiting all day long, I might lose my mind.

Which leaves only one real option and that's not one I'm willing to consider.

"Thank you for the time, Antoine. I really appreciate it."

"Take all the time you need, Tessa, and remember my home is always open to you."

"I will. Merci."

"Bon soir."

I end the phone call and toss it to the coffee table. Earlier today, I convinced Sawyer and Debbie to go out. His training camp starts on Monday which means the season will soon be in full swing. They not only need the night out and time to themselves, I need time alone to think. I've ignored the reminder bouncing in my brain from the other night. If I move in with Jason, I'll have lots of alone time to think. And also, time to snoop through his cupboards and sniff his clean laundry. Not that I'd do that. Or roll around on his bed and sheets when he travels. That'd be gross. And strange and only massively creepy. I haven't thought about doing any of those things. Ever.

No, what I need is exactly what I'm doing. Watching a drama with hot firemen on Netflix while enjoying a glass of red wine, the bottle on the coffee table for easy refill convenience. It's only slightly ironic one of the paramedics on the television show is fostering a secret crush on a fireman and has for years. She doesn't remind me of anything or anyone.

If only Jason hadn't offered up me staying with him as an option, this might be an easier decision, but even Sawyer and Debbie seem to think it's a great idea. Assuming I get the job, I can try it out. If it doesn't work out, I can always move back to Toronto, probably beg Antoine for my job back or something similar if I want to. I can keep my apartment and pay rent while living here rent free so when I'm ready, I can ditch the lease and do something here.

Debbie has it all planned out in a bulleted list of pros with not surprisingly, nothing in the con column.

This woman. She's a witch. Every time she mentions me staying close, she rubs her belly. She's an only child and she's been with Sawyer for so long she's like my older sister.

I want to make her happy.

I just want to do it without the risk of causing severe bodily harm to the Ice Kings best winger or further damage to my already banged-up heart.

However, all of this could be talk and a disappointment if I don't at least apply for the position. I grab my laptop where I've already started updating my resume and pull it onto my lap.

Hot firemen on the television are momentarily forgotten while I update my tasks and duties and qualifications. I've done some research on what a travel director for sports teams do and talked Sawyer's ear off last night, so I feel pretty confident I can do the job.

It's not in marketing and that might set me back if this doesn't work out long-term.

Do I even want it to work long-term?

Let's not even get me started on the things Jason said to

me the other night, or the way he so easily offered to let me MOVE IN WITH HIM! He's lost his mind. Taken one too many pucks to the helmet. Smashed one too many teeth.

He and all his growly *I'm tired of waiting* sexiness is saying all the things I wanted to hear years ago and instead of falling into his arms, confessing my unending lust slash maybe love for him, I'm more terrified of him than I ever have been.

"This is ridiculous," I mutter, crafting an email to one Ms. Sylvia Kuznetsov. "I should hop on my flight on Saturday, get back home and sort myself out."

With an air mattress and a need to go shopping since all I own now is currently in a carry-on suitcase in my brother's guest room.

Sighing, I take a sip of my wine and stare at the blinking on my screen. With each passing moment, I swear it starts talking to me. *Do it. Do it. You know you want to.*

I take another sip of my wine, set it down, and quickly finish the email to Sylvia. My brother gave me her email as soon as Jason left the other night and it's been staring at me on the nightstand. I'm pretty sure it's been talking to me, too. Whispering coercive language while I sleep at night. I keep falling asleep thinking this is the worst idea, and waking up thinking it's the best idea *ever*.

I'm so mentally screwed up. But I hit SEND and slap my laptop closed without waiting to ensure the email went through. I'll leave it to fate. I've just slid it back to the coffee table and refilled my wine when a knock comes on the door.

Frowning, I consider ignoring it. I don't know anyone and since Sawyer took his car, he'll be able to get in through the garage. Plus, if there was a problem, he'd call.

"Tessa!" I jolt at the sound of my name coming through the door, muted by a voice I know.

Jason. He's here. I stand on shaky legs and darn him for affecting me from so far away with only my name being shouted. He knocks again, louder this time, and I yell back, "I'm coming! Keep your pants on!"

I flip open the door and am met with the cockiest grin smiling back at me as Jason's hands drop to the waistband of his navy cargo shorts. "I suppose I could agree to that. But wouldn't it be more fun with them off?"

I slam the door back in his face but he's too quick for me, because of course he's too fast. His livelihood depends on his reflexes. He throws up his hand and the door slaps against it right before it can smack him in his previously broken nose. "Cute. Invite me in."

"No."

"Why? You scared?"

Of him? Uh. Yeah. *Duh!*

"What do you want, Jason?"

"Talk. I only came by tonight to talk."

CHAPTER ELEVEN

JASON

IT OCCURRED to me over the last few days I made a gross overstep when it comes to Tessa's life. In my defense, I pretty much steamroll over everyone and everything when it comes to getting what I want. Granted, it's usually related to hockey and becoming the best on the ice. I keep pushing Tessa even when I try to step back. It's simply not in me to take my time and be patient when it comes to what I want. I've debated for hours since practice ended if I was going to come here. As soon as Sawyer mentioned he and Debbie were headed out for dinner and a movie now that she is feeling better, all I kept thinking of was Tessa.

And the fact she's alone. For *hours*.

While Tessa gapes at me like a fish, frozen to her spot, I take advantage of her shock and step through her brother's front door and curl my hands around her shoulders, gently placing her to the side so I can enter.

She's standing in front of me in a pair of black sweats

that bunch at her ankles and a pale pink tank top with straps so thin I can see a strap of her bra peeking out from beneath on her shoulder. Her hair is piled on her head and I don't think she has a speck of makeup on because I can see freckles dance across the bridge of her nose.

She's also never been sexier.

"Tessa."

It comes out on a groan and since she's still gaping at me, I step forward. Another step. I move slowly, give her time to realize what I'm about to do and she either wants it as much as me, or she's in some serious shock.

I reach out my hand and slide it to her neck where her pulse vibrates beneath my palm.

"Jason—"

"Don't tell me to stop."

She blinks, long light lashes flutter wildly and I keep moving closer to her until her breasts brush against my chest and her back presses to the stairway behind her. "We... this..."

"It's happening. It'll be okay." I'm sure part of her is scared. But there's nothing here in front of me that's saying she doesn't want this. I've waited too damn long. I want a taste. Just one little taste of her to see if all the chemistry I've always felt is in my mind or real. That's all this is.

A chemistry test.

I tilt her head up until she's forced to meet my gaze. My free hand curls around the banister behind her. I've caged her in and while her claws are sheathed, I take my chance.

I press my mouth to hers and in an instant, a wholeness I haven't felt in almost a decade suffuses everything together in my system. This, this is what I've spent years waiting for. For Tessa, her mouth on mine, the taste of her red wine on my lips and the flowery scent of her perfume invading my senses so strongly a rumble builds deep in my gut and bursts from my throat, straight into her mouth. I part her lips with mine and *freaking hell* she succumbs, stops fighting the kiss, and begins to participate.

Her hands fly to my hips, fingers dig into my shirt, clinging me to her but this woman... she has to know there's nowhere I'd rather be. Unless that other place is us closer together, clothes flying off until there's nothing left between us.

My dick is hard, a throbbing incessant need in my shorts, and I roll my hips forward until she can feel the hard length against her lower stomach.

Yes. She feels even better against my body than I imagined she would and I've done a lot of imagining over the years.

Her mouth yanks from mine and her eyes fly open, blue pools of lust blink back at me and she breathes out my name. "Jason—"

Pretty sure we aced that test.

"It's okay," I tell her because her eyes are wide and she's gasping for breath but there's a wild fear swirling in the look too. "You feel this though, right? You feel it, too?"

She blinks rapidly. Lashes flutter across her cheekbones while she stands inches from me, mute.

This isn't even what I came for but I can't be sorry about it, either. Still, I force myself to regain control and while she still stands so close and unmoving, I place a gentle kiss on her forehead before resting mine there.

"You don't have to say anything. I didn't come for this but you're irresistible."

"Jesus," she whispers and I laugh. And I think she means God, so I tell her I'd prefer if she called me that which earns a soft laugh from her.

Exactly what I wanted.

"If I step back are you going to bolt to your room and lock the door?"

"I was thinking more about chugging the rest of the wine over there." She points to some place behind me.

"How about instead of that, we hang out and talk?"

"I think that seems equally dangerous as what we just did."

"Funny. That didn't feel at all dangerous to me. It felt perfect."

"Shit, Jason. Give me a minute to process this, okay? A week ago I didn't even know you had these thoughts or feelings for me and now everything's changing so fast."

"I'm not really a tap the brakes kind of guy," I admit.

"Well I'm not really a full steam ahead kind of girl, so you might have to compromise here."

I chuckle and kiss the top of her head again. "Point taken. Although I don't really do that well either."

She pushes against my chest and I give her space, but before she can slide away from me, I take her hand and guide her to the couch. She collapses onto the couch immediately like her knees have gone weak. I smile as I refill her wineglass. I made those knees weak and I'm pretty damned proud of myself for it.

"Thank you," she says, taking the glass from me.

I head off toward the kitchen where I know the rest of the wineglasses hang and grab one. When I return to the living area, she's reseated herself on the couch and I take in the way she's sitting. Knees bent and feet propped on the couch in front of her. Ankles crossed, one hand wrapped around her legs. She couldn't curl herself any tighter into a ball.

I give her the space she's basically begging me for with her body language and sit on the far chair.

"You might not actually believe me based on what just happened but I came over tonight to apologize for pushing you too far the other night at dinner."

"Okay."

"Okay?"

"Sure." She tips her head to the side. The mess of her hair on top of her head flops along with her. "I'd like to hear you apologize."

I sort of thought that's what I did and for a moment I don't speak until Tessa starts, "Dearest Tessa, I'd like to humbly—"

I lift my hand. "I get it." Quirking an eyebrow, I ask, "Dearest, though? Really?"

"If you're going to do something, might as well be the best at it."

I chuckle and take a sip of my drink and set it on the table next to my chair. Clasping my hands together, I prop my elbows on my spread knees and lean forward. "Dearest Tessa, I'd like to humbly apologize for pushing too hard the other night. Maybe announcing the job wasn't the right time. Maybe throwing out the idea of living with me wasn't right."

"Maybe?"

"I suppose you and I won't know unless we try."

Blue eyes narrow on me into slits and she takes a drink. "Why now?"

"Because you don't have Will. Because you're here. Because I've wanted this a long time and barely held myself back on New Year's and I felt like a serious asshole for that afterward since you were engaged. But now... now, I don't want you to leave back for Toronto without at least making it clear I'm interested."

Her limbs slowly loosen until she's not wrapped around herself like a pretzel anymore.

"I don't know what to do about any of this." She flips her hand in the air. "The job, moving... I still need to figure out all that crap with Will and that obviously sucks, by the way. And then there's you... and Sawyer."

"I'll handle Sawyer when the time comes." I'll handle Will too, if I ever see the loser, face to face.

"When the time comes?"

"Well I'm not going to wait around tonight and tell him I want to shoot my shot with his little sister, if that's what you're asking. That'll get his fist slammed into my face."

"You know I *am* an adult. I'm not sure we have to tell him anything."

"He's my best friend. I'll tell him. He'll hate me if I don't, but that doesn't mean it has to be right away either."

"You make this sound so easy."

"I don't think anything between us will be easy. I think our emotions run high and we'll fight a lot and we'll snark back and forth and we'll disagree about movie choices and restaurants to eat at. I think we'll fight a lot."

"Well, don't you make this sound fun."

"Oh. I'm getting to the fun stuff. I think that all means we have a lot of passion between us and when we unleash that... that will be explosive and fucking beautiful. Much like that kiss was. Plus, I've always heard make up sex is hot sex."

She blushes then and loosens her limbs further. I take the chance and stand and take my wineglass with me while I move to sit next to her on the couch.

"You want this, don't you? At least tell me I'm not the only one feeling this. That I haven't been the only one…"

"You haven't." A rush of a laugh bellows from her and she shakes her head. And God, she's beautiful when she's nervous. "Damn it, Jason. You're not even playing fair here right now. This is unexpected. So crazy. It's all my teenage dreams come true and that's terrifying as hell."

"Want to tell me about those dreams?" I tease. "Maybe we can reenact some of them."

She chokes on the wine she's just sipped and slaps my shoulder. "No. No way. You're never knowing those."

"No?" Damn, she's beautiful. Even with all this mess of hair and nerves she still has balls of steel and a fiery attitude I don't even want to tame. I want to see how hot she can burn. Stroke the embers. "I could tell you some of mine."

CHAPTER TWELVE

Tessa

THIS GUY. I'm not sure what to do with him right now. Kick him out? Pull him close? My pulse is thrumming in my veins making my whole body feel alive and antsy. And here's Jason, sitting close, smelling so good, and looking so much better.

I now know what he tastes like and it's so much better than anything those teenage dreams I've had of him could come close to.

"No. I don't want to know those." I mean, yes, I do. Tell me *all* of them, Jason. Tell me the dirtiest ones. The ones that repeat in your mind. The ones you go to when your hand is all you have. Obviously I want that. Obviously I like hearing all these things come out of his luscious, kissable mouth.

But is it smart?

He chuckles and shakes his head. Like I'm cute. But

really! He thinks I'm cute! And beautiful! I should be doing backflips in my brother's living room right now.

Gesturing to the laptop on the coffee table, he asks, "What about that job I mentioned? Have you given it any thought?"

Only every single second since he left the other day. "Yeah." I hesitate how much to tell him. He clearly came here with a goal, but I'm still not sure our goals align even as fantastic as he makes the possibility of us sound. "Yeah, I well... I emailed Sylvia my resume earlier. Right before you got here actually."

"Yeah? So you do want to move here?"

"I don't know what I want yet. But I do really like the idea of being close to Sawyer and Debbie, especially with them having a baby."

He grins, leaning back into the couch. He's put space between us and my psychotic brain doesn't know if I'm thankful for it and want him to lean in. "Crazy shit, isn't it?"

He looks almost as happy as I feel at the thought of Sawyer having a baby and for a split second, all my worries and fears evaporate into wordless bubbles in my brain.

This... this guy right here, grinning up at me, happy for Sawyer... these are only a few of the reasons why I love him so much.

But giving Jason a chance? A real one? Despite the kiss that almost made my knees give out earlier, despite his words and his boldness... giving him a chance frightens me.

How much do I have to lose if this goes sideways? He's been a part of my life for so long, and embedded in my heart for almost as long, what will I have left, if this doesn't work? I'd rather have him in my life as my brother's best friend than not at all.

I think all of this, about all of the cons and pros Debbie

wrote down earlier this week and blurt out, "I hate the winters in Toronto."

Jason brings his glass of wine to his lips and hides his smile. "Yeah?"

"Don't get cocky. I also really hate the heat and humidity." He gives me a look, and I smirk at him. "Don't say anything about how you can get cocky. Grow up."

"Oh, it's up. Almost always is when you're around."

I choke down my wine and shake my head. "You can't start saying things like this to me."

"The truth?"

"Yes. Actually that's a great idea, let's go back to you *not* saying the truth. I think I like that version of you better."

"No you don't." His head tips to one side along with a chunk of that hair I'd love to get my hands on. "I think you're more scared of this version."

"Psssh. I've already said I'm not afraid of you."

He smirks. "And I know when you're lying. I also know when you're nervous, you fidget with your left earlobe."

I open my mouth to say something, but yup. Sure enough, my left hand is at my ear, tugging on my earring. "That doesn't mean anything. My earrings make my ears itch sometimes." I drop my hand to the back of the couch. Then my lap and then drape it over my stomach. Good grief! What do I do with my hands?

"Okay." It should be criminal for people to be so damn good looking. I'm momentarily stunned by the simple beauty of Jason as he leans in, and his hand reaches out, brushing a chunk of my hair behind my ear. His fingers linger there making obvious goosebumps erupt on my neck.

"Nerves and fears aside, Tessa, do you want this?"

What? His body? Hell yes I do! And no. Will has left some parts of me chipped and marred and I'm not sure I trust myself to make any rational or sane decision right now. Case in point: the way I'm already leaning into his soft touch.

"I like the idea of being close to Sawyer," I admit. It's not like I never considered it. But back when he was early in his career, the risks of him being traded was too high. I didn't want to bounce around two countries following him, but he's settled here. He's older. What would happen if I *did* do this?

"And me." Jason's hand skirts to the back of my neck and gosh, he's so warm. So firm while being so soft at the same time. His voice alone makes my knees wobble. Thank goodness I'm sitting down. The heat from his hand spreads down my chest, straight to my heart until we're connected. I try to move away from his closeness, the seriousness in his chocolate brown eyes, but his hand on my neck stops me. "Do you like the idea of being close to me?"

Yes! No! It's the fact I can't seem to even know what I want right now that makes this such a bad idea. "I don't think that's a good idea."

His head dips down and I'm forced to meet his gaze. His eyes are narrowed, inspecting, beautiful and full of emotion and every terrifying possible thing. "No?"

The tremble of my body and the hitch in my breath belies my words, but I press on. If he knows me as well as he claims to, it's obvious to him.

"Will—" I say on a ragged breath. I'm trying to think clearly to explain, but every part of my body is pulsing. It's the same reaction I've always had to Jason, even back before I truly understood it. I only knew he made me feel good. But now, it's not *good* I'm feeling...

"Will's a dick."

"Yeah, well, I love him and stayed with him for way longer than I should have, so what does that say about me?"

"It makes you loyal," he says and then he moves closer until his mouth is near my ear. My breath stalls and stops and stutters as I feel his warm breath skate across my cheek, my jaw. "It makes you someone who hopes for the best in others, who doesn't give up. It makes you a woman who will fight for what she believes in and all of that, Tessa, all of that is sexy as hell."

"Jason—"

"You need time, I can give that to you, but I want to give you that time while you're staying with me so we can explore this possibility without the fear of Sawyer at every second."

I need space. He can hypnotize me with his eyes and the masculine scent of his cologne so easily my mouth seems to be opening to agree with him. There isn't a single part of him that isn't dangerous to look at and I swear those eyes are magic, luring me in to do his will.

"I'm not moving in with you." I know the risk if I do. I'll forget the fact I'm trying to rebuild my life and I'll jump into bed with Jason, let him have his wicked way with me, *show* me all those fantasies he mentioned earlier and then I'll screw it all up because I'm still messed in the head over a douchey ex.

"So, you want to stay here, listening to Sawyer and Debbie go at it all the time while watching her puke? Don't you think they should have this time alone?"

I scowl at him. It's possible a growl leaves my lips too. "No, I do not enjoy hearing any of that. But on the plus side, I'm getting lots of running in."

"Yeah." His gaze drops to my stomach, my hips, and my

legs. "I noticed that. Your legs, Tessa... I can't wait to have them wrapped around me."

I cough and sputter. I need more alcohol. Perhaps I've had too much and I'm hallucinating this whole thing. I'll wake in the morning with a killer headache and the memory of these wild, crazy dreams.

"You're evil."

His eyes pin me to my spot. Gone is the teasing, gone is the fun-loving guy with his cocky smirks and salacious grins I want to lick right off his face. "I'm honest, get used to it. So, my place. You can stay there. Figure out your life and what you want to do next, and I swear to you, if what is best for you is heading back to Toronto, we can have a conversation about what that will look like if you want me in your life when you do. I don't want to pressure you, Tessa... I just want the opportunity to know if the reality of you is as good as I've already imagined it."

"Again, you make this sound so easy."

"I think it only has to be complicated if we make it that, but it doesn't mean it'll be easy. It might take work, but I already know you're worth the effort."

"Jason." Tears bubble in my eyes and burn. I'm not so sure he's right about that.

"Don't cry. Let me show you how confident I am in us, even if I have to prove it to you."

CHAPTER THIRTEEN

Tessa

I'M ARMED with my duffel bag and my work laptop bag as I step off the elevator in Jason's building, key to his penthouse condo in my hand. He gave it to Sawyer at their practice today and said I was welcome to move in whenever I wanted.

Which really means I've spent the evening debating on whether or not I was going to do this. And why am I doing this? So why am I hesitating? Why am I shuffling outside his door like a toddler who needs to pee and needs to pee *now?*

On one hand, this is Jason we're talking about. The guy I've loved since I can remember and now there's an actual chance we could become something more.

On the other hand... what if it doesn't work? What if we don't work? Then I'll have to suffer a loss of a dream and a hope that I've always wanted. This has the potential to crush me worse than anything Will could have done to me.

Come on, Tessa. This is Jason freaking Taylor. *And he's made it clear he wants you. All you have to do is knock on the door or use the key. Everything you've always wanted is on the other side of the door.* Literally. Me. Living with Jason Taylor. The guy I've loved for as long as I can remember who has recently hinted at having these same feelings for me.

Granted, he hasn't used that dreaded "L" word, and for that, I'm thankful. I'm pretty sure it'd make my head explode and all that would be left of me is brain matter splattered all over his walls and floor.

The keys jingle in my hand but before I can use it, the door unlocks from the other side and opens.

And here he is. In all his beautiful, freshly showered and looking so lickable in a pair of sweat shorts that hang past his knees and a black T-shirt.

"Hey."

Jason reaches out and I freeze. He smirks, casually taking my suitcase handle from my hand into his and lifts it across the threshold. "How long were you planning on standing here, debating on whether or not you wanted to do this?"

I hate that he knows me so well. "I wasn't debating."

"I've known you were at the door for five minutes. Doorman said you were on the way up."

"There were lots of people on the elevator. It took a while."

"This elevator only goes to two floors."

Right. I knew that. His floor and the one above because he has one of the only two penthouse condos in the entire building. It was a fast elevator ride. Also, the elevator was totally empty. Still, Jason knowing I'm nervous about this isn't exactly something I want to have happen, so I'm willing to lie through my teeth and I won't back down.

My suitcase is now placed in his entryway, sitting on his gorgeous dark wood floor. Jason himself, all that dark hair swept to the side with his cleanly shaven jaw is still at the door, holding it open, giving me plenty of room to enter.

One foot in front of the other. It's all I have to do. One simple step and then I'm in his place. It's not like I've never been here. He's lived here for years. He's thrown parties here when I've visited. But we both know this is different.

Still, my feet are stuck. Rubber flip-flops firmly implanted into the navy blue carpet of the hall at my feet.

"I'm not going to attack you the moment you step inside, Tess."

I roll my eyes. "I know that." Flinging back my shoulders, I enter his place and then a quiet breath leaves me. Like I was holding my breath out of fear a bomb would go off as soon as I stepped foot inside. Instead, nothing.

The massive television is on with a movie or show I don't recognize and its volume is low enough I can't hear it. Surrounding the television large enough to fit inside a movie theater, are soft brush dark brown leather that looks more suede and oh so comfortable. His entire condo has been decorated, professionally, because I remember six years ago him bitching about how the woman wasn't listening to a damn thing he wanted.

I also overheard him tell Sawyer she became much more cooperative once he slept with her.

The door behind me closes and then Jason's next to me, hand at my shoulder, lifting and tugging my laptop bag's strap off my shoulder and placing it on my suitcase. "What just pissed you off?"

"Nothing."

"Then why is your face all scrunched up?"

Ugh. "It was nothing."

I move to step around him but his arm shoots out, palm pressing to my stomach stopping me. I don't react. Honestly. His hand on me doesn't send a shiver through my entire body making it entirely obvious what a simple touch from him does to me.

"You're lying."

"I'm not." My teeth grit together. Okay, so he knows me well. Does he have to keep shoving it in my face?

"You are. Talk to me."

"If I don't, will you decide this is a horrible idea and send me back to Sawyer's?"

"No." He leans down, dark brown eyes alight with something that sends a rush of heat somewhere south of my stomach. "But I have ways of making you talk, if you think you're ready for that."

I am most absolutely *NOT* ready for that.

"Right. Because your kisses make women who won't listen to you suddenly malleable, right? Or maybe that's your dick."

"What the fuck?" His hand falls from my stomach but he moves forward instead of away from me. I've gone too far. I know this. I need to learn how to censor my thoughts around him, but this is who we've always been. We've sparred like I'm the annoying little sister and this whole time, he's been shoving his dick in other women and I simply am not prepared to explain why this makes me so furious.

"You know what? This was a mistake. I should never have agreed to this. To any of it." I'm barely inside his place and we're already fighting. There's no way this will ever work and it's safer to cut my losses. I go to reach for my bags but Jason blocks them, kicking backward with one foot and sending my suitcase wheels sliding farther away from me.

"Don't even think about it," he says and I swear he's getting growly. Instead of turning me on though, this time it makes me mad. "What in the hell was that for?"

"What? The reminder of how you get women to do what you want them to?"

It's fear making me act like a lunatic. Maybe a side of jealousy.

"Jesus, Tess. What in the hell are you talking about?"

My teeth are snapped together so harshly my jaw aches from the pain. I don't even have time to answer, not that I'm planning on it, before his hand is wrapped around my arm and he's yanking me forward into his place. I trip over one of my flip-flops and stumble as he drags me into his living room and it's not until I can see the full expanse of his wide open living and kitchen and dining space that my anger boils over. Someone else decorated this place. Someone else chose every single stupid, impersonal knickknack and color scheme. *Someone else* chose that stupid jersey that's hanging on his wall with the gorgeous freaking frame and the highlight articles surrounding it, artfully arranged so it's eye-catching and not some stupid cocky show of how awesome he is.

And that *someone* has slept with him. She carries around the knowledge of what he feels like moving inside of her.

And I'm me... stupid, naive Tessa who gets screwed over by every guy she's ever dated.

"Talk."

"No." I'm throwing a tantrum. To top it off, I throw my arms across my chest. He can't make me talk if I don't want to.

"Tessa—"

"You slept with her!" The words fly out of my mouth before I can stop them and my eyes grow so big I fear they might fly out next.

"What?" He jolts back like I've slapped him and his anger melts away. It's impressive, really, to watch him go from irritated to surprised... to... I don't know what this new look is. "What are you talking about?"

I throw an arm out. "Your designer. The woman who made this place look so nice." And God, I remember overhearing that conversation like I remember the very first time I met him. *"Woman wouldn't listen to a single thing I said. Kept shoving black and red down my throat even when I said I hated it. Finally, she got my dick in her mouth and she started listening a whole lot better after that."*

It's humiliating. I remember every single word I heard and the only part that was gag-worthy about any of that was hearing Sawyer slap him on the shoulder and say, "Way to go, man. Gotta do what you gotta do."

They'd laughed.

I slunked away from my parents' basement where they'd build an indoor skating lane for Sawyer to practice. Then I'd gone to my room and cried and avoided Jason the rest of his visit.

Now, he's in front of me again, black brows pulled together and he's chewing on the inside of his cheek. "That was years ago."

I can't even look at him. Shrugging, I hug myself. I'm standing here revealing way too much. "I know."

"You can't still be pissed about that, Tess. That was, what... six years ago?"

Seven. But who's counting. Not the loser and fool I am. I stay quiet and press my tongue to the top of my mouth. It should stave off the tears that are building. This was stupid. So stupid.

He dips down until he's directly in my line of sight and when I slide my gaze toward his kitchen, his hand comes up, cups the side of my neck and guides me back to him so I have nowhere else to look except his beautiful face with his flushed cheeks and hard jaw and raised cheekbones.

It's criminal how pretty he is.

"Every time Will touched you, I wanted to rip off whatever finger he had on you and break them, one by one, in multiple places. You were engaged, Tessa, and you think that didn't piss me off? I could tell how big of a loser he was and I had to sit there, doing *nothing*, and watch that play out and you're throwing a fit over some designer I fucked once or twice years ago?"

It's not like I don't realize how stupid I'm behaving. I shrug in response.

Jason smiles.

The jerk.

"Why are you smiling?"

"Because as insane as this entire stupid conversation is, you're jealous, which means you care. And frankly, it's fucking hot."

"I'm not—"

"Lie to me again and I'll kiss you."

My jaw snaps shut. He grins again and waves his hand in the air.

"Throw all the shit away. Burn it for all I care. Now, should I show you to where you'll be sleeping?" My brain spins as much as my body when he brushes by me, heads toward the hallway and barely glances back. "You coming?"

CHAPTER FOURTEEN

JASON

I'M FEELING PRETTY DAMN happy with myself as I grab Tessa's suitcase and carry it down the hallway. There's no way she'd lash out with such jealousy if she didn't want me as much as I want her. Seeing it in action though, is something I never thought I'd see. It confirms we're doing the right thing here.

We need this time and as much as I want to keep walking, take her suitcase to my room and my closet and unpack her meager belongings right next to my clothes and move in together, I know that's about five hundred steps further along than where we are.

Hell, I can barely get her to admit to liking me or stepping foot into my home.

Throwing her things in my closet and then Tessa herself onto my bed might be pushing it a *bit* too far.

I'll wait for her to be ready but that doesn't mean I'm not going to play dirty to get her there, either.

Her footsteps catch up, and I grin at the floor, knowing it took her awhile to follow me. I stop outside one of the three guest rooms I have. My parents usually use this room because it has its own private bathroom unlike the other two rooms that share the bathroom in the hallway. My brothers usually stay with Jude since he has the largest house so one of those guest rooms is set up like an office. The other room has my gym equipment in it for when I don't feel like putting in a full day's workout at the practice facility or in the building's gym.

My decorator, whose name I don't even remember, didn't touch this room, but my mom added her own personal touches over the years like photos of her and my dad, some of us four boys when we were all little kids wearing hockey helmets that made our heads look three sizes too large for our bodies.

When I asked her why she did all this stupid crap in *my* house, my mom shrugged, and went back to dusting her own space. "We travel a lot. Between the four of you boys all over the country and spending so much time traveling with your dad, I like these rooms to feel like mine."

Now I'm wondering what fit Tessa will throw when she's sleeping in the bed my parents sleep on, falling asleep with a pic of me at ten holding my first State Championship trophy propped up on her nightstand.

Scratch that. No one needs to see that. I grab the photo and tuck it face down in the bottom drawer before Tessa makes it into the room.

I've already settled her suitcase on the bed and I hear her quick hitch of a breath when she reaches the doorway. It's not like Tessa's never been here before. She's come for parties and get-togethers, mainly ones I plan when she's in town so I can spend time with her in my space, but I'm not sure she's ever ventured into the bedrooms.

"This is beautiful," she says, eyes scanning the white bedding, the pale blue walls. It has an ocean feel with the light wood and thick white carpeting. I think it's way too girlie.

Mom loves it. It's not a surprise Tessa does, too. It's feminine and a far cry from all the dark browns and blues out in my main living room.

"Mom's done most of it." She's added faux green plants over the years and some brass colored decor things like balls sitting on a platter, a metal globe. Some weird arrows she hung on the wall.

I long ago stopped asking her why. When my mom comes to visit, she takes over.

We love her for it. She's been married to a former NHL player for forty years, has birthed and raised four of her own boys who have all gone on to the NHL even if my oldest brother is now retired and living with his wife and kids in New York. Frankly, with all the work she's put into my own success over my lifetime, she could hang a life-size cutout of David Hasselhoff and I wouldn't say anything.

A blush grows on Tessa's cheeks almost as if she's embarrassed by her behavior earlier, maybe my need to reassure her the decorator didn't touch this room. Since I won't lie to her about that, I say nothing.

"Aren't your parents coming soon?"

She still hasn't actually entered the room. Maybe she has some room threshold crossing fear I've never realized. Or she's more nervous than she needs to be.

"Pre-season next week but they're already planning on staying with Jude and Katie. Katie wants her help with wedding planning stuff."

"That's exciting, your brother getting married, isn't it?"

"I'm happy he's happy. And soon it could be Sawyer."

"Right." Her smile falls and she shakes her head. I feel like a tool. She was supposed to be getting married next summer as well, although I'm not exactly upset about that one. "Everything... everyone's changing. Fast. I'm not sure I'm keeping up."

"People grow and change. It's life, Tessa."

"Yeah."

"You going to come into the room at any point in time tonight or sleep in the hallway?"

She laughs, shaking her head, but I notice how her hand goes to her left earlobe again. She always tugs that ear when she's nervous.

I give her space. The last thing I want is her nervous, but I get it. I haven't exactly beaten around the bush with what I want from her but that doesn't mean I'm jumping her tonight.

Although I *want* to. Definitely.

I step toward the closet instead of reaching for her like I want to and throw open the door. "This is the closet. Hang whatever you want. The bathroom is there." I gesture to the other closed door. "Make yourself at home, Tessa."

"Well yes, me and one small suitcase will be able to manage." Her face scrunches, unhappy.

Every time she thinks of Will and makes this face, I want to punch him even more.

"I've got money, you need or want to go shopping."

"Oh no. No, no, no." She shakes her head and waves her hand in the air. "You are not buying me a wardrobe. And Debbie's already offered."

"You'll take help from them and not me?"

"Well, yeah... but I don't want to have to take it from them either."

I have to resist throttling her. Hasn't she learned yet I'd always be there to take care of her? Granted now is in a very different, much less *familial* way than before. But it doesn't change the fact I want to.

Don't push, asshole. Don't push.

"All right. I'm going to let you get settled. Have you eaten?"

She smirks. "Are you going to cook for me?"

"No. But I can have something delivered for you if you want." I hate cooking. I'll deal with a grill if I have to but standing in the kitchen, wasting thirty minutes to an hour just to eat drives me up the damn wall which is why I have a food delivery service that delivers all my meals. Personally, it's handy during the season when I'm always on the go. My fridge has barely more than condiments and beer. Even my snacks are pre-packaged and delivered. Guys give me shit for it, but most of them have women to cook for them because most guys hate it as much as I do.

"Thanks. I'm good though."

"But did you eat?" I get why she won't take help in a massive amount of money to buy new clothes, but is she really going resist letting me order her something?

"Yes. Debbie cooked tonight so I humored her."

"And you survived?" Unlike me who hates cooking, Debbie sucks at it. It's impressive, considering even though I hate doing it I can. It's basic math. Measuring. Pouring. Dumping. Cooking. Somehow Debbie screws up every-thing she tries which is why Sawyer is one of the few guys on the team I know who actually does all of his own cooking.

"The lasagna noodles were hard to choke down but she was feeling better and had energy, so I did my best."

I laugh. I can only imagine. I've had food at her house that tastes worse than what I imagine cement bricks would taste like. "Nice of you. I haven't eaten, so I'm going to warm something up. You change your mind, you'll let me know?"

Her eyes have been scanning the room while I talk, like she's trying to absorb everything into her memory so she doesn't notice when I step closer until I'm almost touching her.

I take the opportunity. Perhaps if I move slow while making my intent clear she'll warm up to the idea of this happening faster.

"You'll let me know if you get hungry? Anything here is yours, Tessa. I mean that." Including me.

"Yeah. Okay."

She's still frozen to the carpet barely inside the room and I slide my hand to her stomach, her waist and move even closer until my chest is pressed to her shoulder and side. She smells like fruity shampoo and fear, sweet seduction with a side of sass. There isn't anything about her I don't love. "I'm glad you're here, Tessa. Want you to know that."

"Oh." She jumps as I lean down and slide my lips over her temple. Her body trembles in my hold and I press my fingers against her before letting go.

She sighs as I step back and looks up at me with a dreamy, befuddled expression.

I leave her alone there, smiling at me like that, blushing, and so damn beautiful it hurts not to touch her more.

FRIDAY NIGHT PASSES with me barely seeing Tessa at all. Apparently after she decided to unpack her small suitcase, I then heard the water running. By the time she came out to the living room, her hair was still wet, but in a thick braid that landed halfway down her back. Her face was unwashed and she scurried by me like a nervous little bunny to the kitchen where she ignored me, filled a glass of water, and practically sprinted back to her room.

I gave up on her coming out around ten and irritated she couldn't even bother to act like we haven't known each other for over a decade, I flipped off the television and went to bed.

Where I couldn't sleep because I was pissed at her but thinking of her, sleeping so close to me probably wearing nothing but a tank top and barely-there shorts... or worse... even fewer clothes. I got hard, had to beat it twice to take the edge off before I could finally fall asleep.

Saturday morning went by in much the same way. My one day a week I take as much as I can to sleep in, by the time I did wake up after nine, she'd already eaten some eggs and toast based on the remnants tossed into my garbage can, drank some coffee from my Keurig, and the door to her room was closed.

I ate breakfast and did a quick basic workout in my gym room, refusing to leave until she returned from wherever she disappeared to or unlocked herself from her room. The thought she was actually in there, door closed, ignoring me, made me want to either kick down the door, or take it off its hinges altogether.

Which might be a slight overreaction. I'm in between sets of burpees when she finally returns. I left the door to the gym open knowing she has to pass by here to get back to her room so I see her shadow first and then her legs.

Long, bare legs carrying a sheen of sweat down her defined thighs and calves. I'm not sure it's possible for her shorts to get any shorter, but I am not complaining. The view of her in them is sinfully sexy.

"Tessa," I call out as soon as I see her. I'm not sure if she thought she was getting passed me or didn't notice where I was, but she jumps when I call her name.

"Oh, hey Jason." She grins and laughs. That hand goes to her left earlobe and I fight down a growl that wants to break through.

This woman.

She's killing me. Especially sweaty from her own workout, her braided hair from last night clinging to her shoulder. Her bright yellow tank top is molded to her ample chest.

"What's up?"

What's up? That's what she asks looking like she needs help cooling down in a shower with my hands doing all the cooling down work?

"Are you ignoring me?"

"What? No. Of course not."

Her cheeks, already red and flushed burn brighter.

"So, you didn't hole up in your room last night to avoid me instead of say, have a drink and watch a movie, and you didn't sneak out this morning hoping I'd probably be gone when you got back?"

"Nope." Her fingers go *tug, tug, tug* on her ear.

Liar, liar with the sexy little shorts I wish were on fire so I could peel them off her.

"Cool." I grab a towel from a bench and wipe off my face. "Good. That's good. Then as soon as I'm done here, you can head to the grocery store with me."

"What?"

"The store. We need food. I don't travel for a couple weeks yet and my stuff is empty. Figured you need to eat too, so we might as well go together, right?"

"Um. Well..."

"Unless there's a reason you don't want to go to the store with me?" I throw down the towel. Workout is immediately over. I've barely started but there's another way I want to work out this tension and it doesn't involve push-ups or squats.

She flips her braid over her shoulder, blue eyes wide, bouncing again all over the room instead of at me. "I don't really need to eat."

I laugh. "You don't need to eat?"

"Well, no. I mean..." Her shoulders slump forward and she almost curls into herself. "Fine. I'll go to the store with you."

"Good. I'll be ready in thirty."

"Fine."

"See you then."

"Fine. Anything else?"

"Yeah. One thing."

"What?" She shuffles on her feet and it only draws my eyes to her legs. Trim. Muscled. Hips that curve out with a stomach I know is also toned. To breasts that are larger than a handful, and I have big hands, to the beads of sweat sitting on her collarbone, all the way up to her chin, her nude lips, freckles across her nose.

I skim every inch of her body, prowling closer while she licks her lips and holds her breath.

"You look sexy as hell right now and I can't wait until I'm the one who's made you all sweaty."

Her jaw drops as she gasps. I skirt by her near the

doorway and haul off to my own room, my own shower, before I haul her to hers and prove exactly what I mean.

CHAPTER FIFTEEN

Tessa

HE'S KILLING ME SLOWLY. I'm on pins and needles, jumpy and unsure, and it's all because of Jason with his smooth moves and warm touches and gentle brushes of his lips at my skin. The innuendo, the visions he pops into my brain every time he tells me what he wants to do to me.

I mean, good grief! Can't a recently-broken up with and stolen from girl catch a break? I don't need this insanity in my life right now and yet I'm the one fool enough to walk right into it. Literally.

I stepped right over that doorway last night when I should have hightailed it back to the airport and now I have no clue how to fix this.

Jason's current offense? Being nice. Yes, that's right, ladies. The guy I always thought I know so well is currently driving me mad because he's so much nicer than I ever expected.

"You like asparagus, right Tessa?" he asks at the store

and then throws a bunch into the cart. "And salads, right? We'll get your favorite balsamic vinaigrette while we're here, too." He swerves the cart through the produce section like a man on a mission and that mission is to buy every.single.one of my favorite foods including my childish cake log roll snacks and caramel swirl ice cream and popsicles.

Don't judge. It's hot as Hades here and popsicles are great for hydration and staying cool. I have a feeling I'll need the entire freezer selection if I want to have a chance at calming down around this guy. I mean, my favorite Greek yogurt? Shakes? How long has this guy actually paid this close attention to me, and honestly... it's shockingly weird.

It took me three months to remember how Will likes his coffee and Jason's maneuvering a now overflowing grocery cart through the store with everything I love as if he's been mentally cataloging a list since we first met.

It's madness! It's worse when we get to the checkout and he throws in two gossip magazines because, as he says, "If you're going to hide away in the bathtub again tonight you might as well have something to read."

Then there's the stop at Starbucks with our stocked up groceries enough to feed me for a month—which I'm not even thinking about that yet!—and orders me a large pink drink, because one) they're my favorite and two) absolutely necessary for life and happiness.

Also, joke's on Jason because I'm not going to hide away in my bathtub again tonight like I did last night. And please... I wasn't hiding. I was dirty. What's wrong with a little extra time for some self-care these days? Nothing, that's what. It's not like I took extra special time and care shaving certain areas that have gone unused outside my fingers for the last several months. It's not like I took extra time scrubbing the heels of my feet to ensure my dry skin doesn't scratch his shin hair straight off if I'm ever given the opportunity to snuggle up next to him. And it's not like, I took care of myself in said bathtub thinking of what that would feel like exactly, to be curled up in Jason's strong arms and resting against his massive chest.

So no... there's no way I'm taking another bath tonight.

Nope... I'm getting drunk. And I'm talking, fall down flat on my face, drink the entire selection of fourteen bottles of wine he bought. And yes—fourteen! I went for two. He threw in twelve more and *why fourteen* do you ask?

"It's my lucky number," he said to me with a wink.

Because yeah, all I need now is to be thinking of Jason getting lucky every time I have a drink. Which I certainly won't. Because then, I'm assuming that would mean I'm getting lucky too and as beautiful as the kiss was we shared the other day, as incredible as my body feels every time he touches me, I'm not sure I'm ready for anything that could possibly come next. My heart might explode straight out of my chest with the force of how Earth shakingly magnificent it's going to be.

I want that. But perhaps that's the wine talking, glass number three to be exact, as I sit curled into a ball on Jason's living room couch, watching some stupid movie he put on an hour ago.

See? I'm not avoiding him. We haven't spoken but that doesn't mean anything. I'm enjoying the view of some Chris guy acting all tough and manly by blowing things up and chasing bad guys. Sometimes he even does it without a shirt on and I have to say, this Chris guy has nothing on the man whose couch I'm sitting on.

Jason is sprawled out at the other corner, black shorts on, a threadbare, skintight white shirt pulled on. His arms are tossed across the back of the couch. A glass of water is near him. His bare feet are on the coffee table in front of him and every once in a while I can *feel* him smirking at me out of the corner of his eyes when he glances in my direction, laughing at how I'm tucked into a tiny ball, angled toward the armrest, avoiding him as much as I possibly can while still being in the same room with him.

Suddenly, he gets up. I jump at the sudden movement of his feet hitting the floor, his body rounding the couch. I stare more when his hand settles on my shoulder and his lips brush my ear. "Need a refill?"

"Yes," I croak. My mouth has suddenly gone incredibly dry. I'm parched. I'm hot in places I shouldn't be, and I'm sitting on the top of a bubbling volcano ready to burst into the air and shatter into a thousand pieces.

His laugh echoes over me long after he's gone and there's the clank of the wine being taken out of the fridge, the door shutting. The *glug, glug, glug* as he fills my glass.

I tense, knowing he's going to come back any second, lean over me, maybe whisper something in my ear that'll snap my tightly wound tether. Instead, he rounds the couch easily, my glass of wine held in his hand as he resumes his laid-back, man spreading posture on the couch, the arm near me thrown over the couch and the glass of wine held at his stomach.

"What are you doing?"

He nods toward the massive television screen where again, Chris is half-naked. Why does he have to save the world from imminent doom without a shirt on? "What? I'm watching the movie."

"With my wine. Over there." I point at his stomach. His chest. It's a breathtaking expanse, too large to ignore, too beautiful for words. Like the Grand Canyon. Stonehenge and all those bricks comes to mind.

"Then I suppose if you want it, you'll have to come get it."

"I don't need it that badly. I'm comfortable here."

"Curl yourself into a tiny ball any further and I'll have to give you a back rub to get the kinks all out."

It's not the *worst* thing he's ever suggested.

"While we're both naked," he finishes. If this is his way of getting me to relax, he couldn't be more wrong.

"Or you could come over, sit next to me, maybe act like I'm actually in the room and you *know me*, take your wine, and finish watching the movie with me."

Well, when he puts it that way with my choices, one seems much more disappointing than the other.

It's official. I've cracked.

"Tessa."

It occurs to me I've been staring at his stomach—my hostage held wine, I mean—and drag my gaze up his body to his face. His hardened and beautifully carved face. Has he had work done? It doesn't seem possible someone could be molded so perfectly. "Have you ever known me to not be someone who's going to take care of you?"

One thick brow slowly raises and I hate that he's right. I'm being stubborn and stupid and crazy and it's a movie for crying out loud! With the guy I've wanted to kiss for years. So what! It's not like anything has to happen and I'm not even sure why I'm being so stubborn about this. Or so fearful.

"No," I say, and it comes out so glumly he laughs.

"Come here. I've already told you I can wait. But at least sit next to me and relax a bit."

He does make well-reasoned, valid points.

"Fine," I grumble, because for some reason my stubbornness isn't easily kicked to the curb. Plus, it wouldn't be

Jason and me being normal if we weren't giving each other a hard time. "But I'm only doing it for the wine."

"You keep telling yourself that."

His smile is so blinding I have to squint as I shuffle on the couch. True to his word, he stays still until I'm at his side, my shoulder falling into the curve of his with his arm still draped across the back of the couch. I spread out my legs, straightening them and it takes effort not to groan. Perhaps I *have* been a tightly knotted ball on his couch.

As soon as I'm settled, close to him and against him but not curling into him, he hands me my wine. I take a sip and relax further.

"This doesn't suck," I admit. I'm suddenly five degrees warmer by being close to him and when he shifts his legs, the coarse hair on his scrape the soft skin of my thighs. Strange how that small brush of him against me can be so delicious.

What exactly am I protesting? It's difficult to remember with his pheromones wafting over me, encasing me in an invisible cloud of his cologne and sexiness.

"Thanks," he huffs a laugh and grabs the remote. "I think my company is slightly better than *this doesn't suck* but I'll take it, little miss stubborn."

I scrunch my face up and stare at the television.

"So what movie is this anyway?"

* * *

MY RINGING PHONE wakes me up and I groggily reach for it. There are so few people who could be calling me early on a Sunday morning. I slap the phone a few times before I'm awake enough to grab it and yank out the charging cord.

"Hello?" My throat sounds like it's been scrubbed with sandpaper. Too much wine. Too little water.

"You're going to be my sister for real!" A screeching sound I vaguely recognize blasts through the phone and I frown.

"What?"

"I'm engaged!"

"Debbie?" I pull the phone away from my ear and finally, her words make sense.

"Tessa—"

"Oh my gosh!" I scramble on the bed, shoving pillows this way and that until I'm against the headboard. "Are you serious? You're not joking, are you? Because if you are, this is the cruelest joke in mankind."

"'I'm not joking! Your brother woke me up this morning and asked! I told him I had to call you before he did."

My head is spinning with happiness. "This is wonderful, Debbie! Congratulations! Tell me everything. Well, not everything everything, if you know what I mean, but all the PG-rated good parts I want to hear. How'd he ask? What'd he say? Was he romantic?"

She snorts through the phone. "Please. And I have a better idea. Meet me for lunch? We have a wedding to plan and I need your help immediately!"

A quick glance at the clock says it's only eight in the morning. She's usually bent over the toilet bowl puking her guts out right now. "Are you... do you think you'll feel okay enough for lunch? We can do later."

"No, I'm good. Talked to my doctor the other day and they have some medicine I can take to help and I've felt better. Also, I've already thrown up today so I should be good. So? Lunch. I'll swing by and grab you and we'll go somewhere special. You can have a mimosa for me."

"Or six."

She laughs. "Whatever you need, Tessa. Are you in?"

My brother's engaged. He's having a baby. I might currently be a blubbering, simpering idiot. "Yes!" I shout. "I'm so in!"

"Great. I'll see you at noon. Be ready to plan. Oh my gosh, I'm getting married!"

I laugh so hard my stomach hurts. "See you then, Debbie."

"Sister."

I sniff back more tears. "Okay. Sister."

She ends the call and I hug my phone to my chest. Swiping happy tears from my cheeks, it takes me a full five minutes to stop smiling so hard, remember where I am, and how I got here, because the last thing I remember is sitting watching the movie, going slowly insane and getting drunk. Fall-down, pass-out drunk mission accomplished apparently.

Last night, we watched movie after movie. We didn't say anything. But what I realized is Jason being so close to me is not good for my liver.

Which means, every time he shifted, I felt him. To stop myself from throwing myself at him, I took a drink. His touches became my own personal drinking game. A brush of his hand at my shoulder? Take a drink. A stroke of my hair with his thumb? Take a drink. A shift of his leg that touches mine? Drink, drink, drink...

Which means, he refilled my glass more than absolutely necessary and eventually, between the movie and the warmth of his body, and the stupid manly action movies he insisted on us watching, the last thing I remember is reaching across him to set down my wineglass, settled my head on his chest, and fell asleep with his hand sliding through my hair.

What I don't remember is how I got into my bed. He must have carried me, and I let that realization settle in while I shuffle out of bed and to the bathroom, unsure of how I feel about the fact that I was carried in Jason's strong, bulging arms, and I don't remember how good it probably felt. And I don't remember how gentle he must have been with me to settle me in a bed that feels like sleeping on air and tucked me in without remembering this either. Did he kiss my cheek? Somewhere else? Did he brush hair off my cheeks with his thumb and smile down at me?

Is it possible I've considered this scenario a hundred times or more? Yeah. I jump, startled as I take in my own reflection in the bathroom mirror. My blonde hair is a tangled nest flying every which way. My mascara has smudged beneath my eyes and there are a few pink wrinkles on my cheeks from the pillow. I'm still wearing the clothes I fell asleep in, so I strip them off, step into the shower and scream as a blast of ice cold water hits my naked skin.

Soon, the water heats and I get to showering. Once I'm done, dried off, I take an exceptionally long time blow drying and straightening my hair until it's a glossy sheen down my back and with the towel wrapped around me, I head to the room and then the closet where I grab one of the maxi dresses I brought with me.

Perhaps if Debbie's feeling good enough, after lunch she'll spend the day shopping with me. I can use some more clothes if I'm going to stay longer and especially if I ever hear back about the job for the Ice Kings.

It's still not a job I'm certain I want, but at this rate, I'm not sure the harm either.

Dressed and ready to go celebrate with Debbie, I grab

my heeled, white strappy sandals, compiling a mental checklist of all the things I need to get working on tonight or tomorrow.

Call the insurance company regarding my claim.

Call the police department to see if anything of mine has been found—or Will.

Start searching the job market to see if there's anything else I might want. At least Charlotte is a heavy banking industry. Perhaps I can find a job at a bank designing more marketing brochures like I did in Toronto. Never mind. Not gonna happen.

I cross that idea off the list and toss my shoes toward the entryway. If I'm going to start over, it's going to at least be doing a job I can enjoy. I've been so lost in my thoughts and my ever-growing to-do list I haven't checked my surroundings properly.

Bad idea.

Because the sight in front of me makes me trip on the front hem of my maxi dress and my arms flail, pinwheel style while I correct myself. I do, at the last second, right before I trip onto the wood floor.

"Woah," I gasp, and shove my hair back over my head before I stand.

In front of me is the sight that made me lose my footing, dressed solely in a pair of skintight black boxers and nothing else besides the coffee mug he has in front of his mouth, hiding his smile.

"Everything okay?"

"You should really warn a girl you're prancing around almost naked in your own apartment. It's a hazard."

He laughs and shakes his head. I'm glad one of us is amused by this. I almost broke my nose sprawling face-first onto his floor!

"It's nice to know you like looking at my body."

Please. As if. "I didn't say that."

"But it distracted you enough to trip?"

"Well, geez... it's just a lot of... skin... I wasn't prepared to see."

I ignore him and stare straight ahead while I head to the coffee pot. The handsome naked jerk watches my every step. I'm not an idiot, not completely, anyway. I see him watching me out of the corner of my eye and I most definitely keep an eye on him because one, he's freaking hotter than the sun, and two, because if he makes any moves toward me I want to be prepared.

He stays in the same spot, though, not making an effort to touch me like he's been doing and a part of me is more than slightly disappointed.

Hrmph. I push the pebble of disappointment in my stomach deep down and fill my mug of coffee.

"You look beautiful," he says. "Big plans today?"

In all of his beauty that's scrambled my brain, I've totally forgotten. I spin around and clap my hands together. "Yes! Sawyer proposed to Debbie! They're engaged!"

Before I can stop myself, I fling myself at Jason. I need someone to hug! And this is Sawyer's best friend! "They're getting married, Jason! Isn't that the best!?" I pull back, grinning up at him.

He's smiling down at me. And I've totally forgotten I'm even in his arms.

"He did?"

"Yes. She wants me to help start planning the wedding today."

"Already?"

"Well, a woman gets excited when the guy she's lived with for years finally pops the question."

"That's awesome. I'll call him soon and congratulate him. Did she say how he did it?"

"No, only that he asked this morning."

"Good. Then he took my advice."

"Advice?" Jason's giving proposal advice?

"He said he had some secret planned for her. I tried to remind him Debbie doesn't like surprises."

"Who does?"

"Sawyer—" we both say at the same time. It's then his grin widens and his hands that have been wrapped around me tighten. "Maybe we should celebrate with a kiss?"

He's teasing me. I like it. I want more. And yes, yes, yes, I want the kiss.

"Jason..." I don't know what to say other than his ahem.

"Too late," he says right before he brushes his lips against mine. I inhale a startled breath and freeze and then he's gone, gently shoving me back, and flashes me a wink.

"That wasn't too painful now, was it?"

"Oh. Well, no. Of course not." My fingertips press to my lips. Sealing the kiss in forever? Erasing it so I don't jump into his arms again and slam my mouth to his? I'm not sure what to do!

"Better get your coffee. Sounds like you have a big day ahead of you."

And a mountain of problems to figure out with my life, but somehow, Jason standing in front of me with only his boxers and a smile has me starting to realize that he might not be one of them anymore.

CHAPTER SIXTEEN

Tessa

"CHRISTMAS?"

"Christmas Eve to be exact."

I drain my mimosa. It's the perfect drink after last night and it's my second one today. I need to stop drinking so much. My first excuse is that I have absolutely nothing better to do with my time and my second excuse is the news Debbie just dropped in my lap.

"You want to get married in less than four months?"

"Your brother wanted to elope to Vegas next weekend. Be happy I pushed it out that long."

She grins at me, sweet as sweet can be, happy smile shimmering in the sun almost as much as her gorgeous green eyes. If I didn't love her so much I'd claim she's unbearably happy. As it is, I'm thrilled for both of them.

"Wow. Okay then." I blow out a huge breath and reach for one of the bridal magazines she brought with her. "We should get started then, right? I mean, there's so much to do... I should know."

I laugh awkwardly. I haven't looked at one of these magazines in months. When Will proposed almost exactly a year ago, I was convinced him wanting to spend forever with me also meant he was getting his life back on track. All I had to do was hang in there and I'd see. Everything would change.

Joke's on me though, right? Things certainly changed, just not in any way I could have seen coming.

"Tessa—"

"It's okay, really." I flip my hand in the air and drain my drink. "I'm okay and I'm so happy for you, truly. It hit me when I saw the magazine I was supposed to be planning my own. On the positive side, at least I never started putting deposits down. It'd suck to be out that money, too." Another drink. Another chug. Debbie's shimmering green eyes are no longer shiny but worried. "Although, had I spent the money, it'd be less he could have stolen."

I'm spiraling. This needs to stop. I slap my hand on the magazine and push it to the side.

"We can do this tomorrow or another day."

"No. Nooo. I want this, honestly."

"Are you going to need to be drunk to help me?"

"No." I finish my glass as our server walks up. We're sitting on an outdoor patio, cooled by a ceiling fan on the porch's ceiling and dining on crepes and cute little cucumber sandwiches. It's the strangest mixture of French and English tea time. I love being at La Maison Bistro. Plus, the service is impeccable. All I have to do for a refill is tip my empty champagne glass back and forth and the server scurries off for another one for me.

Across from me, Debbie looks pensive and worried. "Are you sure about the drunk part?"

"Just a lot on my mind. And no, none of it is more important than this. So, let's start planning, okay?"

I grab another magazine and open it straight to an outdoor photo shoot of a couple standing beneath a mahogany stained pergola. Bright, green leaves wrap around all of it with gorgeous white flowers that look too large to be roses falling gently down. It creates the feel of serenity, happiness, and it's breathtaking.

"This is pretty." I turn the magazine around so Debbie can get the full effect, which means I get the benefit of watching her worry for me vanish into a soft, wistful smile.

"I don't know if we could have that in the winter."

"What's the hurry?"

"The baby," she says, and her hand goes to her still unchanged stomach. "I want to be married to Sawyer before the baby gets here and I'd like to have it happen so I'm not huge in the wedding photos. Besides, we've been together so long I'm not sure a huge extravaganza is necessary. We'll have your parents, you, and some guys from the team but I don't need anything huge."

"You won't invite your parents?"

"I'll invite them. The odds of them coming are pretty small, though." She's an only child and doesn't have a great relationship with her parents. Debbie was born in the south and grew up in one of those cookie-cutter neighborhoods with a strict HOA and perfectly manicured lawns. She's said more than once that everything might look beautiful on the outside, but if you lift the roofs, the insides of the homes would show a vastly different, dark and sad story. She came to school in North Carolina, got a job working for a tech company, and never left.

"Okay. So it's small. And I'm guessing it'll have to be inside. Have any locations in mind?"

"Well, that's where I could use your help. Since you're not working, I thought you could help me find some and tour them?"

"I'd love to. So, let's make a list." I grab the notebook she brought and scribble down ideas. Over the rest of our lunch, we brainstorm all types of locations where we could possibly find a venue, on Christmas Eve, with only a few months short notice.

My optimism isn't at its highest levels given the parameters, but Debbie is trusting me with this. And it's my brother. Plus, she's absolutely right. What else do I have to do with my time?

By the time we're done, I'm bubbling with almost as much excitement as Debbie is. We have over two dozen places on the list for me to call and if they're available, we'll scope them out or I will if Debbie is working. We've talked about color schemes, bookmarked magazine pages for potential dresses which will be one of her first stops due to the timing and need of alterations.

I've almost forgotten all about my own problems, excited to finally be thinking of and helping someone else for a change when Debbie leans forward and grabs her iced lemon water.

"So how is it living with Jason?"

I choke down my own water, having switched after the third glass so I could have a clear head to focus on our conversation. Now I'm wishing the water was spiked with vodka.

"It's fine."

She grins knowingly. "Please, Tessa. I'm not stupid. How do you really feel being there?"

"I don't know what you're talking about and I definitely don't think you're stupid."

Her lips press together. "So you haven't had a crush on him forever?"

My senses tingle, tiny little needle pricks run up my arms. "If you thought that, and were worried about me living with him, why in the world did you practically force it on me?"

"In business, you know, we learn that if someone answers a question with their own question, it usually means they don't have a good answer in the first place."

"Debbie—"

"And I *encouraged*, not forced you because I thought it'd be good for you. So spill."

If I could reach her across the table, and if she wasn't carrying my precious niece or nephew, I'd throttle her. Wrap my long fingers around her tiny throat and squeeze painfully until she chokes. "It's fine."

"Fine?"

"Ugh. I hate you."

She balls up her napkin and tosses it at me. "I'm your favorite and you know it so don't deny it. So spill, come on. What's it like?"

The instant urge to defend and hide my feelings for Jason cling to the forefront, but then I realize, I'm desperate to talk to someone about all my conflicting emotions. All of them. From Will. About work. To Jason. To all the things he's said and the *kiss*. Dear sweet heaven, *the kisses* and the cuddling and his fingers sliding through my hair.

I open my mouth to start and then it all spills forward, rushing from my stomach like I've been holding it back for far too long and now that the dam's been breached, there's no stopping it. I go back to the beginning, my crush as a teenager that blossomed to more. The guys I slept with in college who reminded me of him. Will. Everything.

By the time I'm done, I'm breathless and yet a weight has been lifted. I've never once talked about Jason with anyone because I've always felt it pointless, but now... what if it's not?

"So what do I do?" I ask.

Debbie gives me a funny look for a beat and then throws her head back and laughs. She laughs so hard and for so long, customers at tables start giving us funny looks too. Some laugh quietly as if they're in on the joke. Only I'm not joking.

"Tessa, girl, you kill me. What do you mean, *what do you do?*"

I don't think the question is either funny or confusing. "I mean... what should I do?"

"You're *living* with Jason Taylor and he's made it clear he wants you. What you do is you go for it, no looking back. No regrets."

Well, she makes it sound so darn easy, doesn't she? "My life is a mess—"

"Oh please. Enough of this Will crap."

She's always hated him. Mental note: when everyone who knows you best can't stand your partner, *leave*. ASAP. I try a different tactic. "What if we ruin everything?"

"What if I would have looked at your brother and instead of giving him a chance I thought, 'Oh look, there's that hottie hockey player. He's probably a player and wouldn't want anything to do with some tech nerd like me,' and didn't give him the time of day? But I did. And it was scary as hell in the beginning. Trusting him on the road. The comments about me and him, the comments on his social media pages. There were a lot of times it seemed too hard to be with someone so noticeable, Tessa, but look at me. It was worth the fear and the risk and he did hurt me a few times because that's life. Also, Jason's not Will and he could never hurt you like that. I think deep down, you know that too." She leans forward and covers my hands with hers and squeezes. "It's Jason. You know what kind of guy he is. And now you have your chance. Go for it."

JUST DO IT. According to Debbie, I should become a walking, talking, and sexy little walking ad for Nike and perhaps it was the three mimosas, or the excitement about the wedding planning or perhaps finally unburdening everything I've held so close to myself for so long.

Maybe she's not wrong. I've been thinking of what is the worst thing that can happen if I go along with what Jason's suggesting. What happens if I flip the script and think of the best thing that could possibly happen?

What if I get everything I've wanted when it comes to a man and relationships since before I'd ever had my first real kiss?

I'm dazed as I ride the elevator up to Jason's condo. I have a plan in place. A car ride to consider. A very fast elevator ride that shoots me up to the top of his building to finesse it.

I'll order a romantic dinner.

I'll discuss my concerns.

I'll throw on one of the sexy summer dresses Debbie bought me today when we finally headed out shopping after lunch, style my hair, throw on my makeup.

Essentially, I'll dress to impress and after we've had a glass or two of wine—well me, Jason will probably have a beer. Maybe he'll look even sexier sipping on a single malt whiskey—something expensive, probably. And when it's done, I'll drag my fingertip over his shoulder, smile down at him, and once he's fully surprised that I'm the one coming on to him for a change, I'll lower my lips to his... and then he'll take it from there.

Like Jason knows my favorite Indian restaurant is Tandor's Kitchen, I know he loves one of the local steak-houses when he wants a nice meal out, so I've already called and requested a takeout order via a food delivery app of filet mignon and lobster tails, salads for sides along with aspara-gus, and rice pilaf. It will be *heaven*. Fortunately, it's also only a block away from his condo, so hopefully it arrives as scheduled in exactly one hour, nice and warm. Which gives me *just* enough time to start part one of my plan.

Showering. Knocking his socks off with my sexy little black dress and slamming hot lipstick.

See? Foolproof.

And it'll end with me seeing stars and loose limbs after finally... finally... Jason and I spend hours exploring our bodies with our hands, our mouths, and connecting in other, even better ways.

All of this means I can feel the grin stretching my cheeks as I open the door to his place, already planning my undergarments so I'm completely shocked as I kick off my shoes and slide them under the entry table as Jason always does to find him in the kitchen, closing the fridge with one of his pre-made meals in his hand.

"Stop!" I cry, and my bags are abandoned at my feet. He stares at me and I run to him, slapping away the plastic container. "Don't eat that!"

It splatters to the ground. I gape at the upturned black plastic bowl before peering up at Jason.

Instead of the shock I expect to see, he's giving me a curious expression, lips upturned at one corner. "Was there something about my salmon that offends you?"

Umm. I roll my lips together before letting them pop loose. "Well, yeah."

I hadn't considered the time I was arriving back. I for some, stupid ridiculous reason hadn't even considered the fact he'd be home and well, hungry, when I returned. We stayed at the restaurant for hours and then did some significant damage at the mall, in part because Debbie kept stopping at every single baby clothing store and bought out the entire supply of gender-neutral clothing along with decor for the walls and newborn infant toys. Then we took a break for protein smoothies when she started feeling tired and a bit nauseous before finishing our mall ravaging and her extravagant spending at the department stores.

I had no clue Debbie can *shop* and she's not even in prime form right now.

Still, none of this explains my extremely bizarre behavior.

Jason crouches down and picks up his meal, checking to make sure nothing has spilled. "Care to explain?"

Well now that I've just acted like a lunatic, I suppose I have to.

"I ordered us dinner. It's coming in an hour and I don't want you to spoil your appetite."

"You could have simply said that instead of assaulting my food."

Sure I could have. He should know acting sane and rational has never been a strong suit of mine.

I shrug. "Probably."

"You're acting strange. What are you planning?"

"Moi?" My hand goes to my chest.

"Tessa."

Somehow, my name sounds like a curse and I scowl at him. "Nothing, okay? I'm not *planning* anything except a dinner. From Maple's Place."

His dark brows shoot up, lines crease his forehead. "You planned a dinner from my favorite restaurant? Tessa... that's not necessary."

His voice softens as he speaks. I can picture his mind, adding up the cost of what I probably purchased because if I'm getting food from his favorite place, I'm definitely going to get him his favorite foods.

"Let me do this for you," I plead and I hate the begging tone in my voice. It makes me feel small. Pathetic. Because he knows my funds are minimal and he's obviously noticed the massive number of bags I dropped. Pretty sure they shook the floor. But Debbie was generous and insistent on pretty much a whole new wardrobe. Also, it's impossible to say no to a newly engaged, happily pregnant woman.

His gorgeous dark eyes crinkle at the edges. With a voice smooth like honey and as sinful like dark chocolate, he says, "Okay Tessa. We'll do Maple's."

CHAPTER SEVENTEEN

JASON

TESSA'S DEFINITELY PLANNING SOMETHING, only I haven't yet been able to suss out what that plan is. From her strange behavior as soon as she stepped into my place to her disappearing act shortly after I agreed to her dinner idea, I've been left alone to try to figure it out.

Only, she gives me nothing, but a quiet pleading tone that practically begged me to allow her to spend way too much money on a dinner and left me with no idea how to proceed during this night so I don't screw it up again. Is it simply a thank you dinner for allowing her the freedom to stay here?

Is it something else? Please, for all that is good and right in the world, please let this be the night she realizes how much she wants me. I want absolutely nothing more and if Debbie spent that many hours with her this morning, I'm hoping like hell she helped Tessa get her head on straight.

Preferably with that pretty head aimed in my direction.

There's also the chance it's a goodbye dinner. Although the bags of clothing give me hope she's planning on staying, what if she's simply replenishing her wardrobe before heading back to Toronto?

The uncertainty has me on edge when I finally hear the door to her room open. I'm standing in the kitchen having a beer and wishing it was something stronger as I wait for her to appear.

"Holy shit." I'm dumbstruck at her appearance and my arm slowly lowers to the counter.

Her blonde hair is curled, loose waves bounce and sway over her shoulders as she heads toward me. Her face is tipped toward the phone in her hand, thumb swiping over the screen which is a shame because it means I don't get the incredible appearance of her eyes or the rest of her face, but I'm pretty sure she's doing this on purpose. She's in a skin tight black dress. It looks sleeveless, just a whole lot of skin showing along with her cleavage before two thick straps angle up to her throat and disappear behind her neck. Jesus. It looks like someone ironed the fabric onto her, melted it straight against her skin it's so damn tight to every single one of her beautiful curves, and then forgot the second half of the fabric because this dress ends only a few inches past her ass.

Her feet are strapped into the sexiest pair of black sandals I've ever seen, fabric or ribbon threads that criss-cross over her feet and wrap around her ankles, almost up to her calves to a dainty bow tied at the back which I can barely see.

She looks dressed to kill and for a night out at the club.

And she's done this for dinner with me.

My dick hardens at the sight of her. I'm vastly under-dressed in my typical shorts and tee I wear when I'm lounging around home, but my skin is overheated at the sight of her. I could be wearing nothing at all and still feel like my body is burning with the need to have her... but more, the need for her to give herself to me.

Just.Like.This.

Shit. Having her come to me like this, a sexy little sinfully delicious package I can't wait to unwrap is better than anything I imagined. And the heels with the bow? They'll be coming off last. Maybe after I'm finished with her.

She doesn't glance at me at all as she sways and steps, so damn steady on those heels it's a miracle and heads straight to the door. The view of her from the back is almost worse. Mostly because the dress doesn't *have* much of a back. My brain is so fogged, suddenly evaporating from my skull and headed straight south I almost miss the look she has on her face as she walks away from me. I catch a glimpse of her cheeks, hot pink and flushed and her teeth are poking out from the corner of her lips.

She's nervous. Trying maybe to act like she doesn't see me eye-fucking her from the kitchen, but she's aware of it.

And I have a feeling my slack jaw and possible drool slipping out of my mouth is the exact reaction she was hoping for.

She opens the door to my condo, thanks someone quietly and when she returns, she's holding three large plastic bags in front of her. Already I can smell the steak and the garlic from the butter sauce for lobster.

While I'm honored she knows my favorite meals like I know hers, the very last thing I want to eat right now is food.

"Tessa."

It's highly possible I growl at her.

She smiles at me, head tilted up, bright red lipstick

staining her lips and a similar heated blush on her cheeks. She lifts her hands in the air, carrying the bags directly toward me. "I have dinner. Are you hungry?"

Oh yeah. I'm hungry like a man who hasn't eaten for weeks. And still... not thinking about food here. She might be trying to kill me. If this is all some *"thanks for the great time see you later,"* game plan of hers, I hope she realizes that will never happen. If so, I'm chaining her to my bed. Hard to run away from this *thing* between us when she can't move.

"Famished." It comes out guttural, leaving her no confusion as to what exactly I'm hungry for. And again. Not for food. "Also, you gotta know right now I think you're fucking gorgeous."

She blinks at me slowly, jaw going slack before she sets the bags on the counter. As much as I want to stand here and keep staring at this bewitchingly insane view of her, I turn toward the cabinets and as she removes our food from the to-go bags, I set up plates and silverware, even going so far as to set out rarely used placemats at the kitchen table.

Something tells me whatever she has planned doesn't involve scarfing down food while standing at the kitchen counter like I usually eat my meals.

Unless later that will mean eating her while she's on the counter.

First things first.

With my back turned, I reach down and give my dick a tight squeeze. I'm hard as a rock and I don't need to be poking out of my shorts while she attempts to continue this ridiculous game she's started.

"Would you like some wine with dinner?"

"Please," she says, and I have to bite down my laugh. This girl. Doesn't she know I don't need all this? Don't get me wrong. She looks fucking fantastic, but I'd happily take her in her running shorts and tank tops and messy hair.

"Red or white?"

Her hand goes to her ear and she tugs. "White, please. I think I have some opened in the fridge still."

She does, so I take out the opened bottle and grab another bottle from the pantry so that can be chilled while we eat. Something tells me she'll need more than a glass or two to get through whatever she's planning.

I don't like games with women. I'm always upfront. I don't typically do the giggly, flirtatious, ridiculous stuff women pull that make them seem younger and less intelligent than they really are. I like women straight up, confident. Sassy and not afraid to be themselves.

But whatever game Tessa is playing? I'm all in. For now, I'm content with waiting to see what she has up her sleeve, if her dress had sleeves, anyway.

I ATTEMPT to keep conversation rolling while we set the table and I bring her the glass of wine. I pour a beer into a glass and take a seat across from her at my table. Normally, I'd sit at the end where I could view the television but I turned that off earlier when she disappeared down the hallway. Not that I'm complaining, the results of her disappearing act are a much better view than anything the television could have on. Yet, she answers me with stilted answers, making my frustration with this game of hers come to a breaking point.

It's possible I've read her wrong. Or maybe she has plans after and none of this is for me? Doubt doesn't come naturally for me. I succeed on the ice based on instinct and learning the feel of others. There's a certain amount of confidence, and yes arrogance, that it takes to make it to the pro level and the reason I'm so good is because I know I am.

I've asked her about lunch. While she was gone, I called Sawyer and congratulated him on proposing and being engaged. We threw in a quick workout at a gym near where he lives and spent a couple hours watching game films from last year's playoffs. With Jude out, we didn't do nearly as well as we wanted to and I'm determined this year we'll bring another Cup back to Charlotte. That means before the season ever begins, we have to figure out every weak spot against our biggest competitors, Boston especially.

I take a breath and relax and stare at the beauty across from me.

Tessa is thoughtfully chewing on a chunk of her steak, much longer than necessary and looking equally distracted.

My gut sours at the thought I've read her all wrong.

"Maple's Place never disappoints," I say, trying to get her attention on me. "Thank you for this."

I haven't realized how much I needed a decent meal until it was in front of me. Filled with all my favorites, the asparagus and lobster and steak are all done to perfection. And man, nothing beats this. My pre-planned meals taste good. They fill me up and give me the nutrition and perfect blend of calories and fat and protein to sustain me for the season, but nothing beats Maple's.

She chugs her wine like it's the last drink she'll ever have. "You're welcome."

I tear off a chunk of lobster and dip it into the buttery garlic sauce. "You going to tell me what the reason for this is? And the dress?"

She chews on a piece of her vegetables and while she

does, blush staining her cheeks further in a way that makes no sense, I take a sip of my beer.

Bad idea.

As I'm swallowing, she looks at me, wide-eyed and blushing and states, "I think we should do it."

I choke on my beer, swallowing it down, but some comes up and burns my nose.

"Do what?"

"This." Her hand flicks back and forth between the two of us and she says, "You know, *it.*"

Not what I was expecting. And not what I wanted to hear.

"By *it* do you mean, you want us to fuck?"

Her bottom lip disappears between her teeth at the corner before she lets it loose again. "Well, yeah."

My silverware clangs to the plate, rattling not only the table and my food, but Tessa. I rest my elbows on the table and lean forward. "Let me get this straight. You ordered this food, planned this dinner, bought that dress looking, by the way, extremely fuckable in it, but you only did all of this so I would *fuck* you?"

Across from me, she pales. "I didn't mean—"

"What? You didn't mean to get all tricked out like that just to get my dick?"

"Jason—"

"Jesus, Tessa. Are you for real? I've been straight up with you about what I want." I stand. I can't believe this shit. I shove back from the table, food spilling off my plate. Who gives a shit. All of this was for *this?* "I might have scared you, pushed you too far too fast, but I haven't hidden what I want from you."

"That's not what I meant. Or what I wanted."

"Then what is it?"

My arms cross over my chest. I'm glaring at her. Needles spike down my spine, irritating the fuck out of me, and more, so is Tessa. Looking so damn embarrassed, her chin wobbles as she sniffs. Shit.

"I thought... you know what? I don't know what I thought. Obviously it's a mistake anyway."

She pushes away from the table, takes off running. On her damn sexy as hell heels through my place and the next thing I hear is the door to her room slamming, leaving me with the utter silence of the shitstorm I've just created.

Shit.

CHAPTER EIGHTEEN

Tessa

IN MY ROOM, heart racing, eyes burning, I flip on the shower and strip off my clothes before jumping into the shower. Alone, encased in the glass enclosure, the water mixes with my tears and I cover my mouth so Jason can't hear me scream in frustration and anger. I stand in the shower, scrubbing my face until my skin feels raw and the hot water pierces my skin like needles. It'll take me more work to remove all the eye makeup I spent so much time trying to perfectly apply earlier.

Thank you, YouTube makeup tutorials.

Also, what a waste.

Stupid. So stupid. I've never felt so stupid.

Or so pissed off. How dare he assume that's all I wanted and then turn into a complete dick when he wouldn't give me a chance to explain. Sure, yeah, tonight was about what he suggested. A little bit, anyway. At least I was hoping that's how it would end. But it's not all I want from him and he didn't even give me a second to collect my thoughts while he interrupted me.

I needed a minute to collect my thoughts. I'd spent hours trying to come up with the perfect way to say, "Hey, let's give this a chance. Let's take our shot and see what happens despite being scared out of my brain and risking ruining everything between us and our families."

Jerk!

I already spent years with a different jerk. A guy who made me promises and told me how much he cared for me and loved me to only then turn around and destroy that trust. The last thing I'm going to do is jump right into something with someone who won't give me a single freaking second to explain myself!

Ugh. Men. Do they all suck so much?

I'm showered off, dressed in a pair of pale pink lounge pants with tiny little glasses of red wine all over them with a matching tank top. My hair is wrapped in a towel and my eyes are red and puffy from crying and all the scrubbing it took to make myself feel clean again when a knock hits my door.

"I don't want to talk to you," I say through the door. There's only one person who it can be and it's the last person I want to see tonight. Unfortunately, he's also standing between me and the rest of the wine I want to consume. How am I supposed to live here *now?*

At that thought, I grab my phone. I'll text the massive, epic failure to Debbie and I have no doubt I'll be back at their place before the sun sets.

"Come on, Tessa. I was a dick. At least let me apologize."

Point for Jason—he's self-aware.

"I don't want to hear it."

"Tessa—"

"No!" My hand grips my phone. I need to get out of here. Stat. "You didn't let me talk earlier and I have no desire to listen to you now. Get over it."

The doorknob turns and ugh. Of course I didn't lock the dumb thing. Right as it opens, my phone vibrates in my hand. I look down and curse.

"Freaking hell. Can this night get any worse?" I mutter. Turning back, I don't look at Jason even though I'm fully aware he's opened the door and answer the phone. "Hello, this is Tessa."

"Tessa. Detective Stroble from the Toronto Police Department."

"Yes, I'm aware. What can I do for you?"

On a Sunday night, nothing good, that's for certain.

"I'm calling to update on what we've discovered regarding your complaint with Will Statham. And unfortunately, there isn't a whole lot of good news I have to share with you."

Of course not. At this point, given how my night has gone, I'm not the least bit surprised there's more bad news headed my way.

"Okay. So you haven't found him?"

"No, that's not it. We've been able to track some of his movements based on the truck we saw leaving your apartment building and someone in your building claiming they saw him moving things out."

"Well, that's not bad news."

"His last known movements based on the credit card he's using is in Nova Scotia."

"What?" I spin, throw my hand through my wet hair and damn it. I totally forgot Jason is still here. At least he's in the doorway, but every muscle of his body looks pulled tight and tense as he rests one shoulder against the doorframe.

Damn the stupid jerk for looking so pissed off and protective when he started this roller coaster tonight. We should still be eating. Drinking. Perhaps kissing and canoodling. I stop that runaway train of thought, glare at him, and go back to trying to ignore his presence.

Which is impossible, but worth the effort.

"I wasn't aware he had a credit card."

"A debit card, actually. From a new account he opened two weeks ago."

"With the money he stole from me?"

"Since it's a joint account—"

"Yeah. I know. It's joint there's no way to prove, blah blah, you've already explained." A shudder wracks my body. I'm not mad at this man. Currently, he's the only man in my life I'm not mad at. "My apologies, Detective."

"Miss Chauncy—"

"Tessa."

"Tessa, no need to apologize." His warm, thick voice softens. It's probably supposed to be his *comforting the crazy person* voice but I only hear his pity.

"So what now?"

"I've placed a call for the local police out there to go talk to him, but I have to tell you, based on the trail he's leaving, I'm not sure there's going to be a whole lot left behind of yours to find. He's been making frequent deposits, small amounts which so far, I'm assuming based on the location of these deposits and their proximity to pawn shops, I believe —with no evidence, yet, mind you—he was selling your items on the way. We can collect it back, but since it might be hard to prove it was just yours and not his, you might have to pay for it."

Like I have the money for this. Or the time. Or the home to put it in.

What am I *doing?*

From the corner of my eye, I see movement and before I can blink, Jason is in front of me, concern wrinkling his brow. He reaches out, hand at my cheek. I lean into it, completely forgetting I'm pissed at him because it's instinct to want to be close to him. His thumb brushes my cheek.

A teardrop glistens on his thumb before he brushes it away.

More tears. I haven't realized I'm crying. Again.

I should be out of tears.

"Tessa," he says, and his voice, so ragged, so heavy it undoes me.

I fall toward him, forehead collapsing against his chest and remember I'm still on the phone when my phone bumps my ear.

"Can I think about it overnight? Call you tomorrow, Detective."

"Certainly Miss Chauncy—"

"Tessa," I mutter but I'm sure my voice is muffled. I'm somehow burrowing into Jason like he's the warmest blanket in existence. Which is silly. He's not at all soft and cozy. He's too muscular and strong.

"Tessa," Stroble says. "Call me tomorrow. Whenever you decide. In the meantime, I'll call the Nova Scotia PD so if you decide to move forward, rounding him up can move quicker."

"Thank you."

"You're welcome. Have a good evening."

"Right," I mutter, and I laugh at the absurdity. Have a good evening. I might need a new detective. This one sucks if he thinks I'm having a good evening or have any hopes of one now.

I end the call and toss my phone to the bed. Jason's arms are wrapped around me, and I can feel the side of his head pressed to the top of mine.

"That didn't sound like it went well."

"Detective in Toronto thinks Will's been dropping and pawning my stuff on his road trip to Nova Scotia apparently."

Two arms wrapped around my lower back tighten. "You going to fight this? Get your shit back?"

I shrug. I have no idea what I'm doing. If there's a point. "I should probably call a lawyer and figure out if it's worth it. Sounds expensive."

"I've got—"

"Don't." I lift my hands to his chest and try to push away but he's too strong and holding on to me too tightly. "Jason. Please."

Go away. Hold me closer. Kiss me. Make me forget. Get out of my room because you're a big jerk, too.

All the thoughts tumble and twist and flip in my brain and I can't finish my thought because Jason's looking down at me. So worried.

So handsome. So beautiful.

All thoughts flee except for the way he makes me feel when he's close to me. The way he made me feel when he kissed me.

I lift to my toes and I'm hesitant. But he doesn't move away. In fact, I think he moves closer, too. And then my lips brush against his, tasting... testing. My spine straightens in preparation for his rejection but it doesn't come.

Instead, he groans my name and slides a hand at my back to my neck.

And then *he* kisses *me*.

And oh sweet dear baby Jesus and all my loved ones in Heaven, thank you for giving me this beautiful gift. He tastes like fresh mint and clean air and as he pries my lips open with a flick of his tongue, I eagerly open for him, surrendering.

Good Lord, this man can *kiss*. My hands ball into fists, gripping his t-shirt, I lean in closer until I can't tell where his body ends and mine begins. Our mouths are fused, tongues tangled and he has me wrapped so tightly in his arms, holding me closely and protectively I never.ever.want this moment to end.

I feel myself being moved, tiny little steps push me backward until there's fabric behind my legs and then I'm falling. Falling.

Onto the bed behind me.

And in love with the man on top of me.

Which is a lie because I've loved him forever and I'm still pissed at him, but this was what I wanted earlier and how I wanted the night to end, so we can talk about everything else later.

Right now I want to feel good and I want to forget the bad. His kisses and the heat and strength of his body pressed to me are going a long way in assisting me in doing both.

I whimper, roll against the heat of his thigh pressed between my legs.

Suddenly, his kiss ends and he pulls back, rolling his own hips into me and holy cow is there a large bulge at my hip. His face shoves into my throat and his mouth is there, breathing harshly.

I cling to him and try to turn my head. I want him back.

His mouth.

His silence. He's so much nicer when he's kissing and not talking.

"Please," I gasp, still breathless from his kisses.

"You gotta know I want this, Tessa. Swear to God, I know you can feel how bad I want this. But not like this."

"Please." I'm desperate. Perhaps that's my problem. I'm too damn desperate. At least lately.

"Tessa. We were fighting. Now you're crying. Will's between us tonight and I don't want that."

"I might always have the baggage of Will. Maybe not between us, but still in my rearview."

"Then that's the risk I have to take."

He kisses my forehead, my cheek, and then the tip of my nose.

Like I'm fourteen years old all over again and I'm the cute little sister.

And that might be what hurts worse than watching him push himself off me, arms fully extended and then he's off the bed, walking away. Closing the door behind him on his way out.

Rejecting me again.

CHAPTER NINETEEN

JASON

I FEEL like an ass for how I handled last night. All the parts of it.

I shouldn't have lost my cool when she approached me at dinner. I definitely should have given her a moment to explain before making her cry and run away from me.

I most definitely *should* have hugged her when she started crying while on the phone with that detective.

But I most definitely should *not* have kissed her. Or pressed my body to the top of hers while making out and getting off on the sweet little sounds she makes when I kiss her.

I also should have ended it, and I meant and still mean every word I said to her. Last night was the *wrong* time to start anything.

Unfortunately, she never came out of her room after and I didn't see her this morning before I had to get to the first day of training camp.

It means I went to bed hard, my hand wrapped around my dick and wishing it was sinking into the sweet pussy down the hall from me.

It means I woke up this morning, hard all over again, wishing I could make things right before I had to take off.

All of this battles in my brain, taking focus from the one —and only—place it needs to be right now and for the next several months.

On the game.

On my team.

Instead, I'm pissed off all over again.

At Will.

I'm pissed at the circumstances that have brought us together.

And I'm pissed as hell last night ever happened.

My mind is not at all where it needs to be and I'm skating like shit. I don't care if it's only training camp and I'm in no danger of losing my spot on the team. I'm too valuable and too good. It's too damn bad that Tessa has sent my sexual frustration running to level maximum. Which again... my own damn fault. Had I not reacted like some giant jerk last night we could have had a much different ending.

"Hey!" That comes from Duke Fletcher, our defenseman and my skates come to a halt, spraying ice all over his lap. "What the hell is going on, Taylor?"

Shit. This is a damn scrimmage for training camp and I've just checked my own damn teammate.

"Fuck. Nothing."

"Bullshit," Hendrix growls at me, getting in my face. "Where's your head? Because it's not here. We're not the enemy today and you've been playing balls to the wall all damn morning." Sebastian Hendrix, one of my closest friends outside Sawyer, rarely gets in my face.

Although I suppose he rarely has a need to. "There're kids here, man." He shoves his gloved thumb in the direction of the boards where after this scrimmage is over, dozens of kids will take to the ice with us.

"I said it's nothing."

"Bullshit." He's not one to let me slide too much and usually I can be pretty honest with him, but in all honesty, as much as I'm trying to act nonchalant with Tessa in my home, I'm walking a thin wire and it feels like it's eighty stories in the air.

This... this is what I need. Someone in my face. Pushing me. Letting me get all my damn frustration out. And fear... because what if she *leaves?*

"Back off, Hendrix."

"No. This is fucking training camp, not the playoffs. You need to chill out."

Around us, it feels like silence has fallen. Pretty sure teammates don't usually throw their gloves to the ice and rip off their face masks and go at *each other* during a team scrimmage. At least, it doesn't happen often. And never on this team. Not since I've been on it.

But hell, there's a first time for everything and Tessa has me so damn screwed up I don't know which end is up right now.

Someone slaps me on the back and I spin, almost shoved to the side by the second line left winger, Pierce Conan. "Off the ice," he snaps and damn. I've made him mad too.

Shit. I should have jacked off before coming here instead of waiting around to see if Tessa would come out of her room.

The problem is I've done that so much since she's

moved in, my dick is almost raw. And whose bright idea was that in the first place? Oh yeah.

Mine.

You're such a dumbass.

Yeah, yeah. I know this. Suddenly all the decisions I've made when it comes to her seems like one giant mistake and if I can't get her out of my head when I skate onto the ice I'm going to be in serious deep shit.

I jump the step as I get off the ice, ignoring the look Coach Woods gives me. I'm pretty sure it's mixed with disbelief and irritation at how I'm not only playing but behaving today and flop onto the bench.

Mikah is next to me and he hits his stick to mine. "What's going on? Pissed at something?"

Yes. Mostly at myself.

Partly because I want to fuck someone into next week and make her *mine*. After last night, it's possible I've royally messed up that possibility as well.

Getting pissed at her for taking a step toward me when it's all I've been wanting?

Then walking away a *second* time?

At this point I won't be surprised if she's either packed up and gone back to Debbie and Sawyer's or if she's on a flight back to Canada.

I grab a bottled water from the holder in front of me. "Nope."

Technically, *pissed* is not exactly the emotion I'm feeling.

"How's Sawyer and Tessa? They find her ex yet?"

"Yeah. They found him. He's in Nova Scotia." With most of *her* shit already gone, pawned along his route and no way to prove the remainder is hers. And okay, this might be why I want to rip off my teammates' heads today.

I jump to my skates and push Mikah's questions out of my head. I need to chill out and get some damn perspective on my job, my life... hell, freaking Tessa.

I roll my shoulders and try to focus on the scrimmage, on Pierce slapping the puck to Newmann with ease and precision but it only holds my attention for a moment. Across the ice, I find Tessa.

She's here.

She's sitting close to Katie and Paisley who's holding Mikah's son, Angelo, but I zone in on Tessa and her curls first.

It's the first time I've ever seen her at one of my games where she's not on her feet, shouting and cheering.

Instead, she has her bottom lip stuck between her teeth, and she's looking at me, uncertain.

Fuck it. The only way I'm going to clear my head of Tessa is if Tessa and I finally clear up everything that's between us once and for all.

Which means once this day is done, I have a lot of shit to right in my life. Starting with my team after today's crap-tastic performance.

And ending tonight with Tessa... hopefully, picking up where I stopped her yesterday.

Screw Will. I can handle her baggage because of him and I can help her get to the other side. But he's taken enough of her life over the last few years and he doesn't deserve to take another minute more.

Not when last night she made it clear she wants me as much as I want her.

ACROSS FROM ME at one of our team's favorite places to hang out, Hendrix takes a pull from his beer before paying attention to me. I've done the practice today. I put in time at the team family party after, fighting tooth and nail to resist the urge to call Tessa and see where she disappeared to. As soon as we could make our escape without being rude, it was Hendrix and Byron who pulled me aside, grabbed a bunch of other guys on the team and demanded. "George's. Now. And you're showing."

It was a demand from the team captain and one I wanted to ignore. Unfortunately, giving them this is the first step into making up for today. My team needs me and my job on the ice needs to become clear.

It won't until I can escape George's Bar, the one place our team can go and hang and have some drinks without being overrun with fans when we need a night to blow off steam or relax. I'm counting down the minutes on the worn and ragged clock behind the bar, waiting until I've put in an acceptable amount of time with the team until I can get to Tessa.

So here I am, most of the guys on the team still giving me a wide berth, the old wood paneling of the walls and floors that stick to the soles of your feet even though I've been here when George is cleaning. It's slightly old and run down, but we're here so often it's most of our home away from homes.

"So, want to explain today?"

Sebastian Hendrix is one of the guys I've played with the longest outside Sawyer. He's been here six years, steady and loyal with a right hook almost as mean as mine.

Still, he doesn't look all that much happier than I am right now.

"Crap day. Shit on my mind." A blonde I want to pull

into my lap, kiss her senseless, and hang on to forever like I should have done last night before I screwed up.

"Please." He huffs and spins his beer bottle. "You're talking to a guy who's seen shitty days. And I know one thing, nothing makes a guy lose his mind—especially you, Mister calm and happy-go-lucky—than woman troubles. So spill it."

"No."

I'm being a stubborn ass, but it can't be helped. I'm not ready to come clean with Sawyer about his sister until his sister and I can figure out what's going on between us. The last thing I need is to cause a rift between us if it's going to end up being pointless.

There's still the chance she can leave. While I trust Hendrix to keep his mouth shut, secrets always have a way of coming to light.

"So there is someone."

"Knock it off. You're the one who wanted me here, so let me enjoy my drink."

"I wanted you here because you were a dick today and I don't want the same shit to happen tomorrow. News is already talking about it. So if you have something you need to get off your chest, I want you here to let it go so we can move on. But shit like today happens again this week and I'll personally tell Coach to bench your ass for pre-season."

Like hell that'll happen. "It's training camp, Hendrix, fodder for media and fans. Nothing that happens there has a bearing on the season."

"For the guys on lines with something to prove, it does. And face it, you're getting old. Maybe you can't handle the pressure anymore."

He's goading me. I still take the bait because fuck that.

"Fuck off." I laugh and take a swig of my beer. Hendrix isn't wrong, but I'm not, either.

Training Camp is mostly to show off our skills, prep the fans for the season. Get everyone riled up and ready so tickets fly off the shelves and arenas are filled. If any question how good we plan on being, if they're not impressed with how we behave this week, it has an effect on sales.

Pro sports are a business. We're a group of grown men who play games for a living and yet the majority of our season will be filled with marketing for the sole purpose of increasing sales and gear so we can keep raking in our millions and making the owner even richer.

It's not skepticism. It's fact. And I'm one of the most expensive sales pieces on the board. They won't bench me unless I'm injured, or doing so rakes in more money.

"No one's taking my spot on the line."

"Conan looked pretty damn awesome out there today. You might have seen that if you weren't so busy scowling across the ice."

He takes a sip of his drink. Nonchalant little fucktwit. He totally knows what I was staring at.

Or should I say who.

"I didn't know you loved me so much to pay that close attention to me."

"I love you enough to tell you to pull your head out of your ass. What's going on with you two?"

"It's Tessa. She's Sawyer's little sister."

"That doesn't mean you can't want her. And you didn't answer my question."

"That's because it doesn't have an answer. Tessa's life is screwed up, I want her. Moving forward is the worst thing we can do with how screwed up things are for her and it also won't stop me. The problem is moving forward and not having it blow up in our faces."

"My advice?" Hendrix asks. He doesn't give me time to answer because *No, I do not want advice.* Although, maybe I need it. "Go for it. You got a chance to have something good in your life, something that could make your life better, you'll never once regret going for it and giving it your all to make it happen. You will regret giving up and not taking the chance."

He takes a large pull from his beer, sucking it back and showing me his teeth while he swallows. His face changes. Something in his expression darkens and he loses that gleam in his crystal clear blue eyes.

"What's going on, Seb?" Sebastian Hendrix has been married to his high school sweetheart ever since high school. He's over his head in love with Madison who most of the team, including me, thinks has become a complete bitch over the years. We try to hide our hatred for her for his sake and all that team morality bullshit, but it's no secret she barely comes around anymore. When she does, the word *pleasant* seems to have been completely removed from her vocabulary.

Whatever look is on his face right now isn't a good one.

"You're not the only one with shit going on right now," he says. It doesn't answer my question at all but when he looks back at me, I swear a chill flies through the air that's how cold he is. "But don't bring your shit to the team or to the ice. Lock it up as soon as you lace up your skates."

"That didn't answer my question."

One side of his mouth twitches. "Madison and I, we have our own problems. That's all I can share. And fuck, she wouldn't even want me sharing that."

My concern for Tessa and whatever is going on in my

own life hops immediately into the back seat. This is Sebastian. Hendrix. Most loyal guy I've ever met. Never looked at a woman on the road. Never so much as laughed at even the thought of a puck bunny. He calls his wife on the plane, on a bus. He calls her when he gets to a hotel, ditches out of an away game nights out at bars to FaceTime her. He'd rather be with his wife than anyone else in the world, he loves her that much. That doesn't mean he's not a part of the team. He's one of the most stable guys we have. Him dragging me out here to try to get my head on straight is proof of that.

"Hey. What's going on? Just because I was a dick today doesn't mean I don't care. You know that."

He's silent for several moments. Long, strained silence where I have enough time to catch George's daughter, Gigi behind the bar and lift two fingers requesting refills. She started helping him out here a year ago, spent three years after her own failed marriage traveling the world, backpacking through Europe. One day, she walked right in on a night we happened to be in the bar with dark purple hair down to her ass, a ring in her nose and a bright, multicolored tattoo of a mermaid and a whole host of other shit down her arm.

George took one look at his daughter, eyes popped open as he asked, "Do I know you?"

She practically leaped over the bar to get her arms around the guy... a major feat considering the size of his gut and the tiny stature of her body... and told her old man to shut up and give her some love.

She lives above the bar and whenever it's quiet and we're here, she can throw her shit around with us with the best of them and her stories about her travels are fucking legendary.

I'm about to give up on Hendrix answering my question, he's been silent for so long when Gigi drops off our beers, clears away my empty. Tonight her hair is shoulder length and hot pink. The mermaid on her arm a teal that shines on her pale skin.

"Thanks Gigi," Hendrix mutters even though he hasn't finished his first.

"No problem, hotshot."

He laughs quietly and shakes his head. "I'm no hotshot," he mutters, but it's not to Gigi, she's already back behind the bar, bar towel thrown over her shoulder as she grabs more drinks for the guys there.

"What's going on?" I ask again.

Hendrix reaches for his beer and spins it in a circle. "Madison and I have been trying to have a baby. For *years*. It's not happening."

Well, that's not what I was thinking. Her leave him? Yeah. That I could see. But this?

"I don't know what to say."

"Nothing you can say. Something's fucking broken and I can't fix it for her and it's killing her. And us. And it's a fucking mess. But what I said before stands true. You'll regret never going for what you want. You won't regret trying. Even if it explodes all over your face into a massive failure."

When he puts it like that... who wouldn't jump in with both feet and risk everything?

"Sorry, man," I say instead. "That really sucks and I'm sorry to hear it."

"Yeah, well, I'm sorry I have to live it. But that's not why I made you come here tonight. You want Tessa, that shit's been clear to anyone with eyes for years except for maybe Sawyer. You want her, she wants you? Who cares the timing sucks? Go for what you want and fuck anything that tries to get in your way."

He angles his beer bottle toward me, and I clink the top of mine with his. "Can I get out of here now and follow your advice?"

"Yeah." He huffs. "Do that. And tomorrow, don't be such a dick to us."

"Promise."

Because come hell or high water, regardless of what comes of tonight, or any future with Tessa, my team needs me and I need to be there for them.

CHAPTER TWENTY

Tessa

I OPEN the door to the building's rooftop deck and am almost suffocated by the blast of hot, humid air. It chokes me almost as my own thoughts have been all day. I've had no idea which way is up or down or right or left since I joined Katie in the bleachers at the training camp today. I sat with a bunch of the wives and girlfriends. Paisley happy to bounce Angelo on her knees and show him off to Mikah. Katie was nervous as Jude took to the ice for the first time since his injury during last year's season. Hell, even Mikah's nanny, Viola, was there, thrilled and laughing with women young enough to be her daughters.

Everyone was in a celebratory mood. Everyone but me.

I sat with Debbie while she carried a pale green hue on her face, silently cheering for Sawyer and watching him skate around, zipping across the ice with his insane speed for a defenseman his size.

Then Jason took to the ice, looking pissed off. Unfocused. Angry with his team, throwing things around when he hit the bench. He glared at his coach, at almost every person who said something to him including Mikah, and I swear at one point he was ready to throw off his gloves and punch his own friends in the face.

And is that what I do to him? He makes me feel like I'm losing my mind, but he's the one who walked away from me. Twice. Worse, afterward, he put in his minimal time with the open skate and then hauled off to the locker room. I begged off the family party afterward even though Debbie insisted I should be there, at least for Sawyer. However, heading back to a quiet apartment that isn't mine and filled with things I don't own only depressed me further and made me more confused.

I belong nowhere. My shot with Jason went down the toilet. I have no idea where I should be or what I should be doing and it's all left me having no energy to go for a run, but still needing fresh air.

So, I finally left Jason's apartment. It took going down to the main floor lobby area, finding a map of the building to find the deck and I almost backed out from the work.

I'm tired. It's late.

The smartest decision I can make is to go back to the bed in Jason's guest room, crawl into bed and not only try to forget this weekend, but reevaluate my decisions in the morning with a clear head. Perhaps the absolute smartest thing for me to do is return home, go back to the job I can at least deal with. I can piece the mess of my life back together without this constant conflict making my head spin. It's causing me heartburn.

Flipping off the long, cardigan sweater I always wear when I'm inside Jason's apartment because he likes to keep his temperature similar to that of the ice rink, I fling it to the faux grass turf near the small dog park. There's a bench nearby so after I pour myself a glass of wine and settle my back against the bench seat, I slide the bottle beneath. My shoes get kicked off to the side and I take the first sip of my wine, gazing at the dark horizon. Shadows and shapes of trees and buildings lit by small glass windows and street lights.

It's quieter than I imagined this area of Charlotte to be. During the day, the narrow, tree-lined streets are packed with cars, the sidewalks filled with commuters and men in suits and women in dresses hustling on their way to work. There is a constant stream of women pushing strollers, college students hauling heavy backpacks while carrying their Starbucks or Dunkin' Donuts coffee cups. But at night, hours after rush hour has settled, the streets are quieter. There's a peace from being able to see it all from the tenth floor of Jason's building.

Unlocking my phone, I pull up a classic rock playlist on my music streaming app, cross my ankles and close my eyes. Other than the gentle hum of cars far below and the whisper of the wind, my music fills the night sky. I will my thoughts to settle. This isn't the first time since being back in Charlotte I've had to disappear to find some peace, and yet, these moments have been the few I've had since I can remember.

Going back to Toronto will not bring me this. But can I stay? I've made a mess of everything.

A whining sound pierces the night and I jump on my sweater-made blanket, twisting toward the sound and then grin.

A man is on the roof and the sweetest looking chocolate lab is leading the way, clearly pulling him toward the park near where I sit. I turn back to my wine and turn down the music. No use blaring it for all to hear when I have company.

As they get nearer, the guy crouches down at the gated entrance to the dog area and unclasps the leash. "Go on, girl."

The dog bounds into the enclosed dog park, grabs a tennis ball already there and flings it toward the far fence.

The man turns to me then, profile lit with the numerous freestanding lamps on the roof. "There was no need to turn the music down on my account. I like Journey."

I grin into my wineglass. "Me too. Cute dog."

Cute guy, too. His body is lean, that of a runner, perhaps a bit of weight on him that shows he might not live in a training room, but he's handsome and when he sits on the far end of the bench where I'm settled, his grin is even more attractive. "Name's Scott."

"Scott?" Well, that's a strange name for a dog. I narrow my eyes and look at the animal racing laps around the fenced-in area. "Looks more like a tornado to me."

The guy laughs quietly and points to the dog. "Her name is Queen, and trust me, she lives up to that completely. No, I was talking about me."

"Oh." I'm stunned. He's polite... no, he's bold and confident. He offers his name and a smile and place near me even though there's room for him elsewhere but he's chosen to be close to me. As if he can't imagine I wouldn't want him near me. "I'm Tessa."

"Just move in? Can honestly say I don't see many women alone up here at night, wine in hand."

"Pity. More people should do it." It's a quip before I realize he's digging for information and possibly flirting?

Gracious. I'm not sure this day can become more weird.

It must be the wine that has loosened my limbs and

tongue. "And yes, I suppose you can say I've recently moved in. You?"

"Queen and I have been here for two years. Good place to live. Nice neighbors."

He flashes me a grin that shows why he's so confident. Smooth operator comes to mind, with his handsome smile, good looks, and easy-going laid-backness he shows in the curve of his body and the way he can spark a conversation without any effort.

And yet, I feel nothing. Nothing but perhaps a surface level attraction to a well-dressed and good looking guy who grins at me like he's willing to happily take whatever I offer.

I turn from him, spot Queen out of the corner of my eye, long pink tongue wagging out of her mouth. She looks like she's smiling as she throws her front paws on a ball the size of a basketball and shoves it away from her before chasing it.

"And I bet you're the nicest neighbor, correct?"

"Well, I wouldn't say the nicest. But probably top five, top ten for sure."

This guy. Scott leans back along the bench, one foot kicked up over his other knee, arms thrown and draped over the back of the bench, eyes skipping between his dog and me.

"Of course, and in a building of hundreds? You must be a friendly guy to make the top ten."

I don't realize how that sounds until it's out of my mouth, too late to suck them back but Scott's eyes crinkle in the way that says he got it. He totally got it.

"If you're new here, I can show you around some. Charlotte has some great restaurants nearby."

Wow. Smooth operator is right. I'm flattered... and yet my stomach is unsettled.

I don't want to go on a date with *this* guy. I want to go

on a date with the guy who I've been avoiding for twenty-four hours since he curled his hands on my shoulders and turned away from me.

It's possible I communicate this thought with my facial expression because Scott's smile fades and he shakes his head. "Ah. I see. So, which one is it?"

"Which one is what?"

"Well, typically, and I mean this in the most sincere way possible, but most beautiful women only turn me down for one of three reasons."

"Wow. You are something different, aren't you?" But this is too good to not hear. I curl my feet up beneath me until I'm sitting like a kindergartner ready for carpet time in school and cradle the glass of wine in my lap. After all, he thinks I'm beautiful. I can give him a few minutes of my time. "How about you tell me what they are and I'll let you know if you're right."

"Oh, I'm never wrong. But okay." He glances at Queen and leans forward, wrists easily draped over his spread legs at his thighs and holds up a finger. "So, one... and it's most obvious, is that she's in a relationship. And before you say you are, I highly doubt this one's your reason or else you wouldn't have smiled back so prettily at first."

"I can't be in a relationship and be kind?"

"Rarely," he concedes. "It happens, but women in love do polite smiles, not wide open friendly ones."

I consider his point. It's ridiculous and slightly arrogant, but since I truly have no interest in him, I play along. "Point taken. And two?"

"There's a complication. You're getting over an ex, starting a life over and you *don't have the time* to give to a relationship right now. How am I doing so far?"

So far, he's two for two. There *is* a guy. And it's complicated.

I take a sip of my wine and shrug.

"And three," Scotts says and leans closer, still several feet away and respecting my space but close enough his mischief is stamped all over him. "Three," he says dramatically and places his palm to his chest. "Is that you don't date men in the building. Too complicated when we don't work out and we have to see each other afterward. You know, when it ends in a fiery crash and we want to rip each other's faces off instead of trying out civility."

"Well, wow... I'm starting to question your taste in women if that's their response."

"So does my mom."

I laugh, throwing my head back and it feels so good. So lovely to be silly with a stranger where things *aren't* complicated and there isn't history.

"So, which one is it?"

"Honestly?"

"It's my preference."

"All three."

"No." His eyes raise like I've said the most scandalous thing and I again giggle, this time while refilling my wineglass. "That sounds horrific."

"It hasn't been a great day, that's for certain."

"Want me to kick his ass?"

"No offense, but I'm pretty sure he could kick yours."

"Ouch. You are bad for my ego."

This guy. He's ridiculous. "I highly doubt that."

I'm about to tell Scott more because sitting with him, the dog occasionally barking, the breeze helping cool the humidity and the wine warming my blood, it feels so *easy*.

I've had so much difficult and drama lately, easy feels... well, tempting.

The door opens to the roof, grabbing my attention and suddenly the cause of all my uneasiness from the night, and let's face it, the decade, steps through, hands to his hips and an expression on his face I can barely make out from here that cools that fun warm feeling I've been having with Scott.

"Based on the paling on your face right now, I'm assuming this guy is yours?"

Jason's not mine. He never has been as much as I've always wanted him to be. And now, I'm not sure he ever will be.

"He's definitely the cause of reasons one and two," I reply.

Scott leans in, still grinning that cocksure smile. "You're right. He could totally kick my ass. But if he needs a good ass-kicking, I'm happy to give it a try."

CHAPTER TWENTY-ONE

JASON

WENT TO ROOF DECK. Be back later.

I'm surprised to find the note scribbled on the back of a receipt when I get back to my apartment. On the other hand, it's Tessa. She knows I'll worry about her if she's not here even if she is pissed at me.

I didn't leave the bar as soon as Hendrix and I talked. I owed it to the guys to stick around and make things right. But once I bought a round of drinks for everyone, stayed long enough to pay the tab for it, I figured things were as good as they're going to get tonight. I'll prove my mettle to them in the morning with our early skate practice.

There's more pressing matters to deal with tonight. I've told Tessa I'll let her take her time and figure her shit out, but the truth is... Will's a dick and she knows it. She might feel lost right now because of what he's done to her, but she'd already broken up with the loser and she was over him before she ever kicked his ass out. I know this because it was back on New Year's where she told me she was unhappy. Granted, I didn't know he was such a piece of scum then or else I would have flown her back to Toronto and kicked his ass then. In fact, it'd only made me happy that she was unhappy.

Might make me a dick for thinking that, but I promised myself that if she ever ditched the dipstick, I'd be first in line. And if I have to be with her while she gets over her embarrassment of him stealing from her, it's a small price to pay.

I think of all this while I throw on a clean set of clothes. Athletic shorts and an Ice Kings gray shirt, my standard wear for when I'm at home, grab the key to my place, and head out to the rooftop.

What I don't expect is what I see when I reach the deck, and slowly, a red haze fills my vision.

She might have been pissed and jealous about some designer who sucked my dick years ago, but that's nothing compared to the sight of her looking up, laughing and smiling so easily with some guy.

Screw being first in line. I plan on being the only guy she ever sees.

Who knows what in the hell I'm thinking as I prowl across the rooftop deck straight toward her, effectively wiping off her smile before I get close enough to see her eyes sparkle.

The guy next to her says something which makes her lips twitch and then without looking at me, he stands and grabs a leash and an ear-piercing whistle grabs a dog's attention that's been lying down in the dog park area, tongue lolling out of its mouth.

"Queen! Let's go."

The dog obeys faster than my dick obeys my silent

commands to ignore the cute expression on Tessa's face as she smiles at the dog.

Perhaps that's what I need. A puppy. A dog to always make her smile so when I'm a dumbshit she has something in the place she likes. I've never considered getting a pet because of how much I travel, but if Tessa's here and she likes dogs...

Tessa stands to her feet, brushing off her backside. "Hey. What are you doing out here?"

"Came looking for you. Thought we could talk."

"I thought we'd said all there was to say."

I glance at the guy who, for seemingly having such an obedient dog, also seems to be struggling with getting the leash on its collar.

I look back at Tessa and arch my brow in question. *In front of this guy? Really?*

"Right," she mutters. "Jason, this is Scott. Scott, this is Jason. My roommate."

"Ah." He winks at her. Fucking winks which makes her hide her smile and turns to me, hand held out and says, "Oh shit. You're Jason Taylor. I'm a fan, man. Nice to meet you."

"You too." Shit. All I need tonight is an energetic fan. I'd be nicer but frankly, I'm kind of pissed he was so close to Tessa, making her smile. Probably flirting. He's a good looking guy. I hate him.

He seems to get the attitude I'm throwing off because he lets go of my hand and holds out his to Tessa. "Thanks for keeping me company tonight. I'll see you around?"

"Yeah. Probably. And thanks too, Scott."

"Not a problem." He steps back and whistles to his dog and heads off with barely a wave in our direction.

Once he's gone, I turn back to Tessa but she's crouched

down, gathering her wineglass and bottle and phone, tucking her sweater over her arm.

"I'm glad I found you out here." She's avoiding me, tucking her hair behind her ear and doing everything she can not to look at me. I'm pretty sure her phone screen is black even though she's staring at it like there's a breaking world news report.

"I needed some fresh air."

Her note said as much.

She skates around the bench on the far side of me and keeps walking toward the door. I hurry to get next to her and before she can argue, I pluck the wine bottle out of her arms where she's cradling it. If I know her at all, as soon as we get blasted with the air conditioning she'll be fumbling with her arms full trying to get her sweater on. Sweet, sexy Tessa in her ridiculous sweater she wears over short shorts and chest-revealing tank tops. I should have known as soon as I walked into my apartment and it wasn't draped over my couch, she was outside. She wears the chunky thing like a robe whenever she's inside.

"So," she drawls out, keeping her gaze on the door across the roof and her arms cradled over her chest. "You found me. Was there anything else you needed?"

You. It's on the tip of my tongue but I suck it back before I can really throw her into a tailspin. This is all my fault. Every single second and now I have no idea how to back up, start over. With all the mistakes I've made over the last week, it's a wonder I've ever been able to get a woman to want to spend time with me. The problem is Tessa isn't just any woman. I care about her. I want her.

Hell, if I'm honest with myself, I've loved her for years. *Years* I spent waiting and as much as I don't want to fuck up the possibility of us, at a minimum I've made the possibility of us getting started a hell of a lot more complicated.

This girl. I laugh at her nonchalant tone. It's the exact opposite of her defensive and protective posture as she tries to stay a step in front of me.

"I came out here to apologize to you for last night. Thought we should talk."

"Which time?"

"What?"

"Which time last night are you sorry for? Being a jerk at dinner or kissing me and then walking away?"

In all honesty, both. I'm not sure she's ready to hear it. Not with how we left things. *Go for it. You'll regret not.*

It's not Hendrix's advice word for word but close enough.

"I'm not sorry for kissing you. I'm sorry for the timing of it, though. And I should have given you the time at dinner to speak before I was a dick. So, I'm sorry."

She stops and spins, eyes narrowed on me. The lights from the building and on poles all over the deck give me enough light to see they're shimmering something fierce.

She tucks her hand behind her ear and her head tilts to the side. "So, what now?"

I should wait until we're back in the apartment. At least inside the building. It's not like I can be recognized out here this late at night, and most of the people in my building are pretty cool when they see me. Hell, I have drinks with a few guys from time to time in the summer.

It could also be smarter to wait until she feels more ready, but screw that. She was ready at least for *something* last night which I've still never given her a chance to explain. And if she needs to heal from the bullshit Will's hand dealt her, then I'm more than happy to be at her side while she does it. But she's sure as hell do it knowing there's men out there—me—who would never treat her to such shit.

I step forward, forcing her to step back until her back's against the brick wall. It's probably hot, maybe scratching her, but that's not why she gasps. No, she does that because I've surprised her and I keep doing it by moving forward, pressing my body against hers and then slamming my mouth to hers. My free hand goes to her jaw and I tilt her head, giving me easier access and it's exactly like the first time I took a kiss from her she wasn't expecting.

She tenses, hesitates, and then she surrenders with a sweet little whimper. I kiss her with abandon. I kiss her because she's Tessa and I can't *not*. Not anymore. I kiss her because she tastes like sweet wine and sunshine and my dick goes hard as I stand here, mauling her against a doorway anyone could walk out of at any moment and still I don't stop.

Who cares about other people when my whole world is in sight in front of me.

I shove my thigh between her legs, and she grinds down at me, making the sexiest little sound when she does. She's gasping. Grinding. Whimpering down my throat and *holy fucking shit* I am not giving her her first orgasm from me against a wall.

Maybe another time though because she's sexy as hell like this.

I slow the kiss, move my leg, and wait until she chases me with her mouth as I pull back.

"What now?" she asks, licking the taste of me off her lips. Maybe she's sealing it in.

"Now, we finish this in my bed."

She blinks. Her eyes are glossy, pupils dilated. She wants this. I can tell and yet she can't hide her fear.

"I'm going to take whatever you're willing to give me, Tessa. But I'm warning you now, whatever you want to give me, I'm going to keep taking until you give me everything. You okay with that?"

"I'm not sure what that means."

"It means, you want sex... I'll give it, but you gotta know now I'm going to start digging deeper so that's not all this keeps being."

She shakes her head. "I don't want just sex."

I kiss her and pull back before we can lose ourselves again. "Like I said. Whatever you're willing to give, I'm taking."

Stepping back, I open the door to the hallway, guide her inside and I keep my hand at her back until we're at the elevator. She shivers as we step inside the elevator when it arrives, hugging her sweater and her wineglass like it's armor.

Silly girl. There's no need to protect herself from me.

By the time we reach the main floor where we have to switch elevators to head back up to my place, goosebumps have peppered her arms.

"Tessa," I say, getting her attention. As soon as we shut ourselves inside the small area, she stepped to the corner, fingers pressed to her mouth and she's stared at the floors lighting up as we descended.

"Huh?"

"Put on your sweater."

"I'm not cold."

"No?" I reach out and trail my finger down her bare arm. She shivers again, this time not from the chill in the air and gapes at me. "Not cold, huh?"

"Nope."

She stares back at the doors. We step out when they open and I guide her to the elevator that goes to my floor.

Once inside, she's so cold her teeth are chattering but I stay silent. She might be nervous. I'm hard as a rock and trying to stay in control. The last thing I want to do is mess this up now.

Halfway up to my place, she throws on her sweater and hugs it to her.

I grin at her.

She scowls at me. "Shut up."

"I didn't say anything."

"Your look says enough."

"Like what?"

"That you think it's ridiculous I can wear a sweater when it's ninety degrees outside."

"Wow. That is some look I have."

"Tell me about it."

I erase the distance between us right as the elevator rings and take her hand. "And what exactly does my look say now?"

CHAPTER TWENTY-TWO

Tessa

HIS LOOK IS MAKING my lady parts stand up and want to dance the tango with abandon. Naked. With Jason. While he's naked too.

And holy goodness, this is actually happening. My heart has been racing since he kissed me on the rooftop and I kept space between us in the elevator only so I didn't throw myself at him. Good Lord, the weight of him against me. It's not the first time. It is the first time he's pressed his thigh between my legs and created friction at my hotspot. Which is also still hot, throbbing, and wet.

Jason's look is absolutely clear in what he wants. I'm still so dumbfounded by what's transpired in the last few minutes I can't form the words to respond to him.

With my luck, I'll open my mouth and only vowels will come out making me look a fool. Instead, I take his hand, allow him to guide me out of the elevator and to his door where he unlocks it. His hand settles at my back and he pushes the door open with his other, effectively bracing me in while guiding me through.

"You have nothing to be afraid of from me."

Ha. Right. I know this. It's not exactly fear I'm currently feeling.

As soon as the door behind us closes, he sets down my wine bottle and gently, slowly, like he's trying not to terrify me, he divests me of my phone and wineglass, reaching out and keeping his dark eyes focused on my face.

Soon, my hands are empty and suspended in the air and probably making me look like a frozen rag doll and he's back in front of me, moving closer. He's done this before, moving with a warning and giving me time to flee but this time, I do the opposite.

I don't want to flee so much as I want to run into his arms and hope like hell he'll never break my heart.

"Jason," I whisper, right before my fingers cling to his shirt and yank him closer.

He has other ideas though because at the last second, he squats down and his hands go to my hips. His legs lift and I have to wrap my ankles around him and adjust my grip on his shirt so I don't fall.

"My room," he says, right before he slams his mouth to mine again and this time, for possibly the first time he's ever kissed me, there's no hesitation. I seal my mouth to his, slip my tongue along his lips and for the very first time ever... *I kiss Jason.*

It's delicious. His lips are so warm, so soft. The scrape of his scruff along my mouth makes me aware of every movement, every moment of our mouths moving together, slipping, sliding, taking and giving.

I have studiously avoided even going near the door to Jason's room on the days when he's gone and I've been here.

I haven't wanted to be tempted or to snoop, and currently when he kicks open his door and flips on a light switch which illuminates two pale lights by his bed, I couldn't care less about anything in his room except finally, *finally* being able to strip Jason down to nothing and let him have his way with me.

"Oh God," I whisper as he pulls his mouth off mine and sucks hard at my neck. I hope he leaves a mark. I want the memory of this night bruised into my flesh for days.

"You taste so damn sweet," he replies and then he's squatting down, setting me on the edge of the bed. I untangle my ankles from his back and my limbs already feel rubbery. Thank goodness he didn't try to set me on my feet. I'd fall straight to the plush carpet beneath my feet.

His hands go to my knees and he pushes my legs open. My sweater is now making me feel unbearably hot. A first. I shove it off my shoulders as his hands move up my thighs, and back down, running his callused palms down my sensitive and overheated skin creating delicious friction.

Peering up at me, his jaw is hard, his dark eyes scorchingly wicked. "I can't wait to taste you down here."

"Please." I widen my legs at the thought. The vision of his dark hair the only thing I see as he goes down on me. I imagine my fingers tangled in his hair, pulling him closer until it's too much and I try to yank him away only for him to insist on continuing.

"Soon." He stands abruptly and I feel the loss of his touch acutely, everywhere, until he's in front of me, whipping off his shirt, shoving down his shorts. He's in front of me with nothing more than skintight boxers that only accentuate the bulk of what is hidden beneath. I don't know where I should focus. His face? The muscles at his shoulders with veins running down his forearms? The bricks of his abs or the flex of his thighs?

I have died and gone to heaven. I'm gaping at him. Sure of it. I have no idea where to explore first when given the opportunity only that I want to memorize it all.

"Stand up."

My legs comply and then I'm in front him, still gaping, still uncertain where to touch him first. It's all my teenage fantasies and then more in the flesh and I'm afraid to blink for fear it'll vanish. I have the undeniable desire to pinch myself to see if I'm dreaming this up but then his hands are at my sides, pushing up my tank top and there is no way I could feel this much if I was actually dreaming.

"Jason." I whisper his name. Nothing else. My vocabulary has fled, but he doesn't seem to mind because he grins at me, raising my shirt until I have to lift my arms and then it's gone, with his hands sliding along my skin.

"You have no idea how long I've wanted to touch you like this. How many nights I've imagined touching you like this. Years, Tess. When it was wrong for me to think this way about you. I've thought of taking you in every way imaginable and that dress you wore the other night? Those damn heels? We're going to re-create that night again. And soon. I'll take you on the kitchen counter, eating you out as my appetizer next time and then fuck you bent over the kitchen table for dessert."

I can picture it. He makes it sound better than anything my own imagination can dream up.

I sway toward him and he halts me, hands slipping to my back, undoing my bra and then the straps are being pushed down my arms.

I have a moment of fear before my breasts fall free, my bra to the floor, and Jason's hands are cupping my breasts, his thumb swiping my nipples as his mouth descends, his gaze on me as he does so. I nod minutely, acquiescing. I'll give him everything. I'll let him take from me whatever he wants and when his mouth closes over my nipple for the first time, the pressure and the heat and warmth from his wet mouth sucking *hard* makes me throw my head back and cry out.

My hands go to where I've imagined them for so long, tangled at his head, scratching his scalp as he plays with one breast before moving to the next and all while he does it, shocks of pleasure are sent straight to my core making my hips move and roll. And he knows, he has to know what he's doing to me because one of his hands is back up my thigh, sliding up and up and up until his fingertips are at the seam of my thigh beneath my shorts, pushing aside my underwear and—

"Oh God, please, yes."

He chuckles against my nipple, continues to work me there and then when he finds my slit, brushes his fingers along my seam, his groan might almost be louder than mine.

"Fuck." He pops off my breasts and lifts his head before taking my mouth. "You're so damn wet and warm."

He's so damn sexy and big and his fingers are still brushing against me while his body moves me backward until I stumble and fall to the bed. His other arm wraps around my back and he catches me, adjusting me slowly before he's on his knees in front of me, hand sliding out of my shorts and shoving them down my legs, along with my underwear. The cool satin slips down my skin and then he flips everything into the air before returning, pushing apart my thighs.

"This might kill me."

"That'd be a shame," he whispers, kissing my thighs,

moving upward. "There are a lot of things I want to do to you but I need you alive for them."

I laugh and I'm a shivering mess. Trembling. So hot. I sit up so I don't miss a thing and watch Jason slide his fingers through my sex, gathering moisture before finally, slowly, dipping a finger inside of me is the most obscenely glorious sight I could ever conjure.

"More," I gasp as his thumb brushes my clit and his finger rolls and twists inside me. I brace my feet on the platform edge of his bed, hands curling over the edge of the covers. My blonde hair falls forward, hiding my breasts so all I see is the top of Jason's head and his fingers sliding in and sliding out of me. The wet sounds it makes as he adds another and then I'm pretty certain this time my groan is definitely louder than his.

He gazes up at me, wicked intentions with promises of delivering an incredible orgasm in his eyes, lips parted, his own cheeks flushed. "I want to taste you and I want to slam my dick inside of you so hard and at the same time, I want to slowly torture you like I've been for so long, and watch you fall apart for me, just like this, with nothing but my fingers inside of you."

I.want.it.all.NOW.

No man has talked like this to me, explained his desires so clearly, demanded he take all the time he wants. Without a doubt, when we're in bed together, it will be Jason calling the shots. I will also have no problems following.

"Jason..." I bite off another cry, teeth grinding into my bottom lip as I stare down at him watching me while his fingers curl inside of me finding that perfect ridge and I arch so hard my hips lift off the bed. He reaches up and pulls out my lip.

"Don't you dare hide those noises from me. I want to hear every single damn scream you have to give me."

And that's what does it. His command, the need he's building like an inferno deep inside my soul, because he continues rubbing, adds pressure with his thumb, and the entire time he alternates between looking at where we're joined and watching my expression.

I shatter. My thighs quake and I grind into his hand. My lips fall open and as I begin to cry out in pleasure, Jason dips his head and takes my clit into my mouth, taking me so far over the edge I'm not sure I'll survive the fall and as he tastes me, mouth sucking my clit and fingers still moving, I fall back to the bed, stomach clenching. My back bows until he drains every single cry from me until I am the one to push his face away from me.

I'm listless, floating on his bed while falling into oblivion and I barely see reality until Jason stands, wiping *me* off of him and he goes to the nightstand at his table, comes back, and drops a string of condoms next to me.

"Can you take more tonight?"

More might actually kill me.

Still, I reach for the waistband of his boxer briefs and echo his earlier words back to him. "I will take everything you give me."

He grins and there's nothing nice about his smile as he kicks off his underwear, grabs my waist and throws me farther up the bed, following me on a crawl.

"Good. Then hold on, Tessa, because I'm about to give you the best ride of your life."

Of that, I have absolutely no doubt.

CHAPTER TWENTY-THREE

JASON

I WAKE up before my alarm and find myself curled and wrapped around Tessa. Her back is to me, one leg curled up and the other straight and one of my legs is shoved between hers. It's exactly how we fell asleep last night. I meant to hold her until sleep took her before moving to my back like I usually sleep but I'm not surprised I haven't moved a muscle.

I worked her hard. Hell, I worked myself hard. I can't remember the last night I've gone so long, fucked so hard. Screwed so slowly. Taken my time and hurried it up. She put me through the wringer and I should be spent and exhausted, instead, my dick is hard, sliding along the curve of her ass. I should give Tessa a break after the hours we spent wrapped around each other last night. I know it's been awhile for her. Longer probably than it's been for me, but still, I haven't been with a woman since early summer.

But holy shit, last night was so damn incredible. Best

night of my life. Even better than winning the Stanley Cup or the day I was drafted. Finally, I've had Tessa. I know exactly what she looks like when she comes, how voracious she is in bed, and it's all so much more damn incredible than my wildest fantasy.

Screw giving her a break. Starting next week, I'm going to be spending several nights a week traveling for the next six months at least. I'm taking all of her I can get before I'm reduced to nights using my hand again when I'm on the road. I already know I'm going to miss her sweet, warm body next to me.

At least now we have time, considering I don't have to be at the arena for a couple hours yet. Plenty of time to reacquaint myself with the feel of her drenched pussy. That thought in mind, my already hard dick twitches against her and I roll to my side so I can slide my mouth over her neck. Even asleep, she's beautiful. All that hair, floral scented all over my damn sheets. Her makeup is smudged across her eyes and her lips are parted, puffy and swollen from all the use they got last night exploring every inch of my body and more than enough time playing with my cock.

God. Tessa's blow jobs are award worthy. Her excitement. Her grow. The way she knows to speed up and slow down and tease me until I almost came down her throat. Fortunately, I'd been able to stop it, but the memory of her mouth on me alone has me groaning against her flesh as I push down the sheet and blanket covering her until her breasts are exposed.

Perfect, pink pebbled nipples ringed with a softer pink. I adjust her, notice she's still sleeping but if there's one way to wake Tessa up, it'll be this.

Perhaps I should add taking her nipples into my mouth to my daily morning routine. The thought makes me smile and I flick one of her nipples with my tongue while watching her, waiting for her to wake up. Her eyes flutter but remain closed and that won't do. I want her awake and needy for when I slide into her.

I roll her until she's on her back and fall between her spread legs. My dick is ready to punch a hole through the mattress and I adjust myself so I don't rub myself off like a damn teenager as I take her nipple in my mouth again. This time, I add my fingers to her sex, playing with her clit. And shit, it doesn't take long before a soft little whimper escapes those swollen parted lips or for her to become wet. Or for her hips to start rocking into my hand.

Her eyes flutter again. Her hand slides down her stomach, coming into contact with my hair and her fingers curl in.

"Yes. Please," she whispers. I'm not even sure if she's awake, but hell, even if she's dreaming I'll make sure it's the best damn sex dream she's ever had.

I turn and kiss her wrist before moving on to her other breast. They're so full, so damn much of them, I could spend hours alone working Tessa's tits with my mouth, my fingers at her nipples. Someday I'm going to slide my dick in between them and watch her catch my cum in her mouth and she's going to love every damn second. Maybe I'll make her get herself off with a toy.

The fucking dirty thought has my mind racing with more ideas. I'm a creative guy. My bet, after last night, Tessa will be willing to try it all with me.

"Jason," she says on a sigh and her eyes are still closed. Her pussy drenched. I want her eyes on me when I slide into her, so I bite down on her nipple and give it a tug, enough for the sting of pain there to shoot another rush of wet down to my fingers.

"Wake up, sleepyhead," I say against her tit. "I need you."

There, her eyes open, lids flutter rapidly before bursting wide open. "Holy crap this is real."

I laugh and kiss her stomach, the dip in the middle down to her belly button while I move my hands to her thighs and then take her pussy with my mouth.

And just like last night, she grips my hair and I suddenly can't wait until it grows out longer. Every scrape of her nails against my scalp spurs me on. Tessa tastes like the sweetest cream on my tongue, something else I definitely plan on adding to my daily diet along with playing with her tits and it doesn't take me long at all before her legs begin shivering, her moans become louder, her grip tightens and her abs contract.

"Close," she cries.

Too close. She'll come with my dick in her this morning, giving me the morning I've waited for since I was twenty damn years old.

"Nightstand," I say, pulling back. Thank God we both slept naked. Her body is on display as she rolls, huffing out a laugh with crimson staining her cheeks. She grabs a condom and falls to her back again.

"I can't believe this is real."

"It's real. All of it." Us. And it's going to be an *us* that lives well together outside the bed, too. That I plan on starting to prove to her every damn night. Tonight, I'm taking her to dinner even if she doesn't know it yet.

I take the condom from her trembling hand, tear it open and then shove her legs wider open, wrapping them around my back while I get situated.

"You ready?" I bend over her, kiss her, slide my tongue into her mouth and press myself at her opening.

"Yeah," she breathes, eyes wide open and on me and this might be my favorite moment of fucking Tessa. Every time I enter her, she keeps her eyes open and there's a moment when they flash and widen, where she feels the full width of me and her body strains to accommodate me. She adjusts quickly and I slide all the way in, taking her mouth while I begin to move. But damn if I don't want to move anywhere and stay inside her like this every waking moment of the day.

Unfortunately, Tessa appears to need me to move too because her hands slide to my hips and she rocks against me, holding on, fucking herself on my dick and damn, that's hot too. Everything about her is sexy as hell in a way so much deeper and just *more* than I dreamed of.

Soon, sweat falls down my spine as my hips piston and roll, finding that hotspot inside of Tessa that makes her arch her back, throw her head back and cling to me while she loses the ability to stay quiet. And soon, she's writhing while I fuck her. Our mouths fuse together and I swallow her cries down to my soul, my balls growing tight and I groan into her mouth, "Get there. Tessa. Now."

Because I'm so close and hell if I'm shooting off before she gets hers.

"So close. I'm close."

"Yeah, baby. Let me see you come for me."

I bow my back, bend down and suck her nipple into my mouth. My other hand goes to her other and my hips move faster.

She arches. Cries out. And then her pussy clamps down on me so hard while she comes, eyes open and staring at me, biting her tongue while she tries to smother her noises. I pump once more. Twice. Three times and then slam inside of her, and empty myself, my orgasm taking over.

And for the first time in my life, I hate the fact there's something separating me from a woman. I want this condom gone. I want my damn seed inside of her. I want her stomach swollen with our kid and I want complete bareness for both of us.

I shove my face into her neck and kiss her shoulder to hide whatever look that thought brings to my face. The last thing I need to do now is scare her off by moving too fast.

I've promised to move at her speed. But hell, I hope she gets to where I am quickly.

Sliding my arm beneath her, I hold her hip and roll us so I'm on my back and she's on top. We stay connected and I hold her close until eventually she pushes up, one hand at my chest. Her hair falls into my face and she laughs, pushing it out of the way.

When I see her face again, she's smiling down at me, biting that lip I waste no time in popping free.

"What's so funny?"

"I guess this takes away any concern of morning-after regret."

"No." My hand goes to her cheek and I lean up to kiss her. "No regrets. Ever."

Her expression softens and she brushes those warm, sweet lips over mine. "No regrets."

Collapsing back on to me, I take her weight and hold her in my arms until my alarm finally goes off.

I tap her but a handful of times. Give it a squeeze until she squirms. "I gotta get up and get rid of this condom. Get ready for camp."

She clings to me like her arms have grown suction cups. "But I'm comfy."

"You want, I can make you more comfy in the shower."

Comfy. I don't think I've ever used this word.

"No way," Tessa says. She lifts her head enough I see a glimpse of her smile through all that hair and then she rolls off me and onto her back. "More sex might kill me."

"Look at you, dirty girl, no one even suggested sex. I just said a shower."

She glares at me out of one eye. "Right. Didn't even cross your mind."

"Trust me. I think if my dick gets any more friction, it might fall off."

"Gross!" She presses her hands to her face and laughs. I kiss the back of her hands before climbing out of bed. "I do not need that visual."

"Don't worry," I call out on my way to the bathroom. "I'll be perfectly healed by the time I get home."

I glance at her over my shoulder. Her eyes do a quick lift from my ass to my face. She looks embarrassed for a second before her grin peeks through. "Sounds like my days and nights have just gotten a lot more busy, then."

"Damn straight. And before I forget... I'm taking you to dinner tonight but don't wear that sexy dress or we'll never eat."

I leave her gaping at me, do my clean up, shower, and when I'm dried off, I stop at the doorway to the bedroom. She's remade the bed perfectly. Nicer than I do it. Possibly nicer than my cleaning company does it. But more, I miss the sight of messy sheets and rumpled pillows and her curled up, naked, next to me.

Later. I remind myself. I'll get more of that later. And hopefully, a hell of a lot more.

CHAPTER TWENTY-FOUR

JASON

COACH WOODS SLAPS me on the shoulder as I jump off the ice. "Nice job out there today."

"Thanks." I rip off my helmet, the chin straps already tugged free before I hit the walkway. Today's practice went a hell of a lot better than yesterday's, thank God. And I gotta admit, I was worried last night's activities and this morning's would make me sluggish.

Fortunately, I played like the King and star I am and never once threatened to punch my own teammates in the face.

I haul off past our coach who's still watching some of the new guys and recently drafted. Some of them will take the ice with us on pre-season, some won't even make the travel roster. Regardless, my spot is secure so I'm done for the day, ready to shower, and then more than ready to see what kind of dress Tessa will be wearing when I get home tonight.

Hitting the locker room, my first stop is to Hendrix. My second to Newman. Both guys kicked ass today too and even though Newman will probably never get Jude's spot on first line now that my brother is back and skating as good as ever, that doesn't mean he doesn't kick some serious ass.

"Nice job, today," I tell Newman, holding out my fist.

"And your attitude's better than yesterday, so we all win." He shoves my chest and I stumble backward, my ass hitting Hendrix's shoulder who's bent over and untying his skates.

"We've talked about this, Taylor. I don't swing that way."

"Dick." I shove his head playfully. "You kicked ass today too. Everything good?"

"Good as it can be," he says.

Last night's conversation jumps to my mind and I want to ask him if something else happened, but I know he won't answer anyway. Not here with all the guys milling around. If he hasn't brought it up publicly, it's not my place.

A loud boom comes from the entryway and all of us veteran players who are already stripping down for the showers turn to see Sawyer sauntering in. His helmet is held loosely at his hand and his grin is a large as my dick. That's to say... huge.

"Hey assholes! Guess who's getting hitched!"

"You finally drugged Debbie enough to agree to marry you?" Jude asks, ripping at his shoulder pads.

"Shut up, asswipe." Sawyer points at him and grabs his crotch. "She's been bewitched by my dick for years. Now she gets it forever. She's fucking thrilled."

Since I've already congratulated him, thanks to my in with Tessa, I stand back and listen to all the other team-mates offer their typical locker room crap and congratulations. Sebastian is the last one on his feet, and he grabs Sawyer into a bear hug. "Happy for you, man," he says, slapping Sawyer's shoulder.

"And that's not all." Sawyer turns to everyone and throws his arms up, spinning in a slow circle. "Apparently my swimmers are pretty damn functional because Debbie's also knocked up. That's right, guys." He slaps his own fist to his shoulder. "I'm gonna be a dad!"

Another round of whoops and cheers go up in the locker room. Next to me, Sebastian's face turns ashen and his head falls forward.

Shit. This can't be easy for him. I press my hand to his shoulder and give him a little shake and when he turns, meets my gaze, I nod. It's the only consoling I can do for him. He takes it, swiping a hand down his face before he backs off.

"I gotta hit the showers," he mutters. He tears off his jersey and pads and I move to Sawyer while he's still getting congratulations.

"Too bad it's season and we can't celebrate properly."

"Fuck that. Debbie's starting to feel better, so I say we all have to go out and celebrate this shit."

"Maybe some other night. Next weekend before preseason games? I got plans tonight."

Sawyer's jaw falls. "You... you're putting off celebrating my baby and wedding for a week? What plans are that important."

Definitely not the time to tell him about his sister. Or what we did only hours ago. Or for hours last night. "Important ones," I say instead.

I turn my back and head to my locker when he calls my name. "How's Tessa doing anyway? She made any permanent plans? Because I gotta say, Debbie's so damn happy she's here and helping her with the wedding stuff."

"She's good." I don't look back at him. "Don't know about her permanent plans though. She'll figure it out." And I'll be there to help her and to ensure things go my way this time.

I get rid of my clothes and pads and take a shower. It's been a long ass day and while it's not even four, I'm in a hurry to get back home, but before I do that, I need to go make another death-defying trip to Sylvia's office. I got an email from her earlier saying there's a stack of gear I need to sign for an online auction starting soon.

I plan on risking her wrath by asking her why in the hell she hasn't called Tessa back yet. If I want to get her to stay here permanently, the least I can do is help her find a job.

Selfishly, now more than ever, I want the opportunity to have her on the road with me as much as possible.

I'M IMMEDIATELY ARRESTED at the sight of Tessa in my kitchen when I enter my apartment. Hell if this isn't something I want to come home to seeing every day for the rest of my life. She's wearing nothing special. Cut-off jean shorts, a simple, white tank top tucked into the waistband. I've already seen her wear them but now that she's been running in the sun, the white makes the tan she's getting seem darker. And over all of it? The damn, chunky gray sweater she's always wearing in my apartment.

She's drinking a glass of what looks like lemonade when I walk in and her smile lights up the whole damn condo and my dick twitches in my shorts.

"Sylvia called me. I have an interview with her early next week."

I can't even take the credit for the help. When I showed up at the marketing department earlier to sign my gear, Sylvia's lights were off and the main receptionist for the floor said she hasn't been in all day.

But now, I'm only focused on Tessa's tan thighs peeking out from those shorts. The memory of the taste of her and feel of her pressed against me.

I drop my workout bag at the door and kick off my shoes before moving straight toward her.

My hands go to her waist and I lift, setting her on the kitchen counter. Her eyes light with anticipation right as I drop my mouth to hers. "That's fantastic, Tessa. I say we should celebrate."

Her hair is curled, loose waves that fall to the ice as she tips her head to the side. "With dinner out?"

"Yeah. We'll get to that."

"Oh." Her blue eyes brighten and her cheeks darken. "Then how do you plan on celebrating?"

As she asks, she runs her hands up and down my arms and her ankles hook at my back.

"Like this." I kiss her, diving my tongue into the cavern of her mouth and tangling my tongue with hers. She tastes like sweet sugar and sunshine, a hint of mint saying she's recently brushed her teeth.

"I like the way you celebrate," she whispers, teasing me, smiling. She's so damn gorgeous when she smiles at me.

"Then you'll like this even more." I step back, putting space between us and my hands go to the buttons on her shorts. I pull them down her legs slowly as she rocks her hips, lifting side to side so I can remove them and then I drop them to the floor while I press one hand to the center of her chest until she's lying down on my counter.

This is just one of the many places I've wanted to take her since she stepped foot into my apartment last week. Once she's naked and exposed, not to mention soaking wet, I take my time eating her until her screams are bouncing off the walls and her skin is flushed and her thighs are clamping down around my head.

And two hours later, I grin as I sit across the table from her at Spagoli's, an Italian restaurant down the street from my building. They make damn good carbonara and I feel like carb-loading for the night ahead of me.

Her hair is still disheveled even though she tried to tame it and every time she smiles at me, I tuck it into my memory bank, adding them up, wanting to never forget a time when I've made her smile.

"How's Joey doing?" she asks, twisting her fork around a pile of her own spaghetti. "Is he looking forward to the season?"

"He's been giving Jude and I shit all week. We play them a few times this year and he's determined this year is their year."

"Vegas has that good of a team?"

"They made some good trades last year. Picked up some promising talent in the draft. In truth, yeah, I think they'll be hard to be beat." I take a bite of food and when I've swallowed, I grin. "But we'll be better. Always."

She shakes her head, laughing at me. I don't care. The Ice Kings are good. We might have gone out early in the playoffs last season but with Jude back, I have no doubt we'll take it all the way this year.

"And Jude?" she asks, like she's reading my mind. "How's he feeling?"

"He's in top form. Looking great. Nervous I think to be on the ice again but that'll fade. Pisses me off our first game is against Boston, though."

"I saw the game he was injured. That was nasty. Selkin should have been out for the season."

"Then I wouldn't have been able to beat the shit out of him when we played them again." She's not far from wrong though. Niklas Selkin is a powerhouse and a major dick. He's had more fines than any player in the league and his ass should have been kicked out of the league or benched far before he took out Jude.

"Yeah, I saw that game, too. I didn't blame you one bit for going after him like that."

This is a surprise. I've always known Tessa hated growing up in the shadow of her brother. With Sawyer's talent and his personality, he casts a large spotlight of attention. So it surprises me that she spends time watching the games. I've always assumed she'd ignored them.

"I didn't realize you watched hockey."

She snorts. "Hard to miss it when you live in Canada. But of course I watch the games, or at least as many as I can. I couldn't miss a chance to see Sawyer play."

"Just Sawyer?"

"Just Sawyer."

Little liar. Her wink gives her away but since I'm enjoying this playful side of her, I don't tease her further. Instead, I switch to her phone call from Sylvia and ask her if she's looking forward to the interview.

"I don't think anyone looks forward to an interview, but the job?" She shrugs and it's not exactly the reaction I'm hoping for. "I suppose maybe it could be a good thing. I guess we'll see."

There's hesitancy in her eyes as she glances at me and back to her plate.

I don't push as much as I want to ferret out all her concerns and worries and solve them for her. Pushing too hard too fast made this all messed up in the first place. I've already made her a promise. If she wants to get a job and stay here, we'll work it out. If she wants to end up moving back to Toronto, we'll work it out.

"How's the wedding planning with Debbie going?" I ask and her shoulders seem to slump with relief that I'm not going to ask about the job.

This makes her smile ignite and she starts prattling on about dresses and flowers and finding venues next week with Debbie and I listen to her every word, not because I give a shit about flowers or venues or even Sawyer's wedding, to be honest. I listen because when Tessa is excited about something, her entire face comes alive and she's magnetic.

As for the rest of my worries, I shove them to the back of my mind.

We'll get there. Someday. We have all the time in the world.

CHAPTER TWENTY-FIVE

Tessa

"YOU'RE HIRED."

"I'm... what?" My hand that was on the doorframe to knock since Sylvia's door was already open, still hangs in the air.

In front of me is a woman, graying hair, keen eyes behind a set of thick black-framed glasses. She's dressed in a black button-up shirt where the buttons at her chest are threatening to revolt against their confinements.

And she... what?

"You heard me. Come in. It's time to work."

"Um." Not to look a gift horse in the mouth, but I'm a bit thrown. "I'm Tessa Chauncy. Here for the interview?"

"You has the job. I'm busy. Let's vork. You vant that, yes?"

I hesitate before stepping into Sylvia's office. She's already as much as Sawyer and Jason warned me about when Debbie and I met up with them for dinner after finally finding a wedding venue for her and Sawyer. It'd been a heck of a long day on Saturday, and Debbie was so tired she almost fell asleep at the dinner table. Because she was tired, I spent most of the meal asking the guys more about Sylvia and the job. They warned me she was gruff. Hard to penetrate.

Sternness is stamped on her features and she gives me a huff I swear is impatience when I don't immediately rush to do her bidding. But what does she expect?

"I'm hired?" I ask, tiptoeing on her carpeted office floor like there are buried bombs in my way. This must be a joke.

She sighs and pushes what looks like a tablet and note-book to the edge of her desk. "I do not have zee time for interviews. You want the job? It is yours. And if it's yours, you vork. Starting today." She peers at me over the top rim of her glasses, chin dipped low. "Unless you do not vant thee job?"

Until a few moments ago, I still wasn't entirely certain. I've spent the last two weeks debating whether or not I want to be in Charlotte permanently and technically, I still have my job waiting for me. I have another week and a half before I have to return. If offered this job, my plan was to give me time to consider it, figuring I could take another week before having to decide.

Things are going so well with Jason. The nights are the best, but the days are pretty great too even though he's starting his pre-season games this week and will begin trav-eling. Something, if I do take this job, I could go with him on trips. There's something thrilling about the idea of being with Jason on the road, watching most of his games live that has me making my decision.

"Oh, I want. Yes, ma'am. I want the job." If I don't take this, another job might not come along, and then where will

I be? My uncertainty about returning to Toronto is based entirely on my relationship with Jason. It shouldn't be, I know this, but things have been so incredible between us, I keep waiting for the other shoe to drop. At least this gets me more money, quick employment and I have a feeling it'll be a thousand times more exciting than working in a bank.

I can tell that by this first impression of Sylvia.

"Good. Then we work." For the next twenty minutes, she rattles off duties for me to do, schedules I must make and contacts I have to call. She gives me the temporary password on the iPad and tells me to go find someone named Emmy to help with the official hiring paperwork to get me on payroll. Then she tells me how much money I'll be making and my jaw drops. Twenty-five thousand more than I make in Ontario.

With the exchange rate, I can't do the math in my head, but it's a significant amount. I'll take that for certain.

She twists her iMac monitor in my direction, clicking a thousand different buttons and clicks of her mouse showing me the system the team uses for scheduling their trips and a million different colored boxes appear detailing which department does what and when.

By the time she's done, I'm ready to quit. Sweat clings to the back of my silk blouse, one of the few nicer shirts I purchased on my shopping trip with Debbie a couple weeks ago.

Among my hurried scribbles on the notebook she provided is a circled note to go do more shopping. Immediately. I had no idea I'd walk in here today and be hired before I could give this woman my name and when Debbie and I had gone shopping, I'd only bought a few dresses, some more casual clothes, that one dress I haven't had the guts to wear for Jason again and one outfit—this one—for an interview.

"There. You are all set and good to go."

I barely manage not to flash her a wide, terrified look before schooling my features. She has to be joking. I'm ready to go? Perhaps to the doctor for as much as my head is spinning.

"Um. Sure."

"Your office is next door. Find Emmy. Come to me with questions."

She drawls out questions like it's a curse word and I inwardly cringe. Sylvia is possibly the most terrifying woman I've ever met. And something tells me if I don't master everything she's shown me in twenty minutes by the end of the day, she'll be looking for another new assistant. If I ever dare actually ask her a question, she'll throw me out on my rear-end.

I jot down a reminder to ask Jason exactly how quickly she goes through assistants on my notebook and stand.

She's turned to her computer and picked up her phone, angrily punching in numbers like she's ready for war and *yeah...* this job is something else. So is Sylvia. Oddly, I kind of like her which might say more about me than her.

I don't realize I've been trembling with nerves until I stand and my ankles wobble. Considering I'm wearing flats and not high heels, that's concerning. Still, I make my way out of her office, listening to her thick Russian accent become heavier the faster she speaks and barks orders to whoever the poor soul is on the other line and find the empty office next door.

Windows. In my office. So much better than a cubicle where the only light I get is fluorescent all day. We're on the third floor of the training and admin facility to the Ice Kings and below my window is the flat roof to what I know is the ice arena where Jason and Sawyer and the rest of the team are having a quick, early morning skate before their first pre-season game tonight.

I stare out at the roof for a moment, the sunshine and the trees. The city. It's so beautiful here. I swear the sky is bluer than I've ever seen in Toronto. I can practically feel Jason's presence... so close...

I grab my iPad and stack of notes and head out to the lobby where I stepped off the elevators only a half an hour ago, nervous and prepping for an interview. Geez. The very last thing I figured would happen today would be actually getting *hired*.

How in the heck can I fill out paperwork when I still have a job?

Just go through the motions today. Give it the day. See how it feels. Make the decision later. That can't be too bad, right? So I take the day, see how I feel. Surely if I decide this won't be for me I can just call and have the paperwork stopped, right?

Sure. Then that's what I'll do.

I head straight to the desk where there's a guy sitting. From only my short time in there earlier before he sent me back to Sylvia's office, I remember his name is Troy. He's older than me, dressed in a navy blue polo shirt with the Ice Kings logo embroidered on his chest. He's on the phone as I walk up, so I take a minute and inhale a deep breath.

This could be a completely new chance for me to start over, creating an entirely new life around family I love and adore, getting the chance to travel, spend more time with my brother. Snuggle my niece or nephew whenever I want. And all of it without the mistake of Will clinging to me like a weird growth.

"Leaving us so soon?" Troy asks, a teasing smirk on his face. Yikes. It's possible working for Sylvia might be really difficult.

"Actually no. I'm hired and she's put me to work."

Troy laughs. "Of course she did. You'll learn, and hopefully quickly, that's how Sylvia is. She wants something, she wants it now, and doesn't tolerate much."

"Well, isn't that a ringing endorsement for my new boss?"

"On the plus side, if you get on her good side, she'll fight to the death to protect you." He drums his hands on his desk. "So what can I help you with?"

"She said I need to find Emmy to deal with paperwork?"

"Ah. Of course. Human Resources is two floors above. Emmy will be in the third office to the right. And congratulations. I'm sure you'll love it here."

It's not like me to take a chance, but in reality, I have nothing to lose. So, leaning in, I quietly ask, "Are you sure? Because Sylvia really does seem scary."

"You'll get used to her." His too-perfectly waxed eyebrows pull together. "Unless... do you cry easy?"

"Not normally."

"Then done." He clasps his hands together. "You should be just fine."

"Thanks. I think."

Later, once I've found Emmy and filled out all necessary paperwork, I'm back in my office where Troy has already called someone from the tech department to come in and set up my computer for the network. In the meantime, I've settled myself in a chair at a small conference table... and holy cow! I have a conference table! This job might be worth it for the awesomeness of my office alone!

I've somehow managed to get through most of the long list of items Sylvia gave me this morning which really entails verifying confirmation of travel for the first few weeks of away games and as I'm checking off item after item, I'm feeling more accomplished. An excitement is thrumming in my veins.

I'm working for the Ice Kings. It's crazy!

It's time to really see if I have a future here, and if so... if this future is what I want for me. Not for Jason. Not even for me and Jason. Or my brother and Debbie, as much as I love the idea of being close to them. For the first time in three years, I get to finally think of no one but myself, and make decisions based solely on what's best for *me*.

"There you go, Miss Chauncy."

I swivel in my chair and smile at Raul, the tech who's been working in my office. "Thank you. Thank you so much."

"Need me to help show you around?"

"I think I can manage it. Sylvia said most of the programs are on the iPad I've been using today. But I can call you if I run into problems?"

"Absolutely. Have a great day and welcome to the organization."

With another thank you, I wait until he's left the office before I run to the chair and spin in circles. A grin breaks out.

I don't even know why I'm hesitating! This job could be incredible. The office certainly is. I have nothing adding up in the *con* column of taking this job except my own hesitation of starting over.

CHAPTER TWENTY-SIX

JASON

THE CROWD IS INCREDIBLE. The energy is electrify-
ing. From the moment I first strapped on a pair of skates,
begging my father to teach me how to skate like he can
when I was probably too young to complete full sentences,
I've never felt more at home than here. We're halfway
through the second period and Jude, while killing it on the
ice, is late with his passes, slow to receive. He's nervous, and
I don't blame him. The game with Boston is just over a week
away and this is his first time back in game mode since his
injury. The other guys are picking up his mistakes. I'm not
worried. My brother's made of metal and he'll shake off his
fears and nerves within the week.

Lights flash. The crowd cheers. Across from me, I'm
getting ready to face-off against Edmonton's toughest
winger, Marx Kauffman. He's burly. Their enforcer. I've
known him since he played for a different university in
college than Sawyer and I did.

"Looking pretty tonight," I tell him through my mouthguard.

Marx is one of the meanest looking men I've ever seen and when he smiles it looks like he's getting ready to eat you for breakfast. "Ready to lose again?"

We lost 2-3 last night in Edmonton. They're always one of our toughest competitors, but tonight we're already up 4-2.

"That's a nice fantasy you have there."

"Actually, what I like to fantasize about is the women who leave you and come to me for something bigger and better."

Normally, his trash talk would roll off my shoulders. He doesn't even know about Tessa. No one does. But still, I miss her like fucking crazy and I'm not about to let him even think of her.

"That's enough—" the ref says, holding the puck up in the air and prepping for the drop.

Unfortunately, for some stupid reason, possibly because I have a head full of a beautiful blonde, Marx gets the jump on me.

"Fuck!" I shout, heading after him as he passes the puck to their center. Fortunately, Mikah Lutzgo is faster and he snags it before it connects, keeping the puck on Edmonton's side of the ice. There are two minutes left in the second period and I want this game over immediately.

Marx has shaken me, not what he said, but what he made me think of all in the span of a few seconds, but I won't let him get me down.

It's been a whirlwind of a few days with the season starting and the pickup from prepping to the insanity of now practically living out of a suitcase always takes a beat to adjust to. I was so exhausted after last night's game I barely had the energy to call Tessa. We spoke for maybe five minutes. By the time we got back to town, she was at work at the team's facility all day. I haven't seen her. It's been twenty-four hours, and I'm dying without her.

Worse, ever since she actually took the job, she's grown quieter. Not at night. When we're in bed, I can still get her to scream the roof down. It's the times when I'm not making her come that she seems to withdraw and it has me worried.

I know she can still leave at any moment, and if she's unhappy or uncertain, I want her to talk to me about it.

Getting her to open up is like trying to pry the top off a can of vegetables without a can opener, and every day it gets a little worse, where I have no idea what she's thinking, what she wants from me. Her. *Us*.

I power through the doubts, skating faster than usual and by the time the second line hits the ice with less than a minute remaining, my throat is parched and my entire body is covered in sweat.

"Nice work out there," I say to Jude who hops onto the bench next to me.

"Slow." His eyes scan the ice, back and forth. He doesn't take his eyes off Newman and this shit has to stop fucking with his head. Much like my doubts about Tessa have to stop messing with mine. I've been going slow, feigning patience, but that shit has to come to an end and soon.

"You'll get there." I punch his thigh. "You've got this, bro. And Newman and you aren't switching, so kick that shit out of your head."

"He's fast. Clean sweeps. Fucker must have worked out double time this summer."

"And you're fucking Jude Taylor. Brother to the best damn winger in the country."

"You're an idiot. We all know I'm better."

And there it is. That's what I've been looking for. His confidence.

"Exactly." I punch his thigh again, hard enough to get through the layer of padding. "We're the best there is."

He huffs a laugh right as the light goes off behind Edmonton's goal and we all jump to our feet as Pierce Conan throws his arms in the air.

Five seconds left in the second period and we're up 5-2 going into the final period.

We win the game 6-3 and when we step out of the locker room into the hallway, Tessa surprises me with her big smile, standing close to Debbie, and tucking her hair behind her ear.

Shit.

I need to talk to Sawyer. The only thing I want to do right now is slam my mouth to hers like most of the guys are doing to their wives who have come to greet us after the win and I have to stand back, looking like a fool.

Yeah. This shit ends soon. I have a girl who I want in my arm. Always.

"Hey," I say, grinning at Tessa as I walk up to her and Debbie. Sawyer's usually one of the last guys out. He has a whole *thing*, a routine he has to make sure he does before and after every game. I quit waiting for him years ago. "You came."

"Work to do, you know?" She smiles at me. Full of shit. She came for Sawyer. Maybe me.

"Ready to head home?"

Next to me, Debbie hides a choking sound. "Sorry, sorry." She waves me off and winks. "Just that that's cute... your home being Tessa's."

The hell? I glance at Tessa who's gone pale. Did she tell Debbie? Or are we that damn obvious? Whichever. I don't really care. I kiss her cheek. "Right. Have a good night, Debbie."

"You too." She wiggles her fingers in the air, sounding like she's singing.

Tessa takes off, walking a step ahead of me.

Normally I wouldn't mind. The view of her ass is a beautiful sight. But tonight it feels like she's running away and that knot of worry in my gut grows.

"EVERYTHING ALL RIGHT?"

Tessa hugs her arms to her stomach, barely looking at me. She hasn't done much of that since we left the arena and she did even less talking in the car after telling me I looked great on the ice.

My jaw hurts from clenching it.

More so when she plays with that damn left ear and gives it a good tug. "Just tired. Sylvia's a hard boss."

"She probably is. I'm convinced under all her Teflon there's a sugary sweet center though."

"Right," she says but she's smiling. At least it's something, even if it fades quickly.

She hurries off the elevator when it opens and is at my door, waiting for me to pull out the key. She yawns as we enter. Who can blame her. It's late, eleven at night and I'm so damn exhausted it's a miracle I could keep my eyes open on the drive home. Usually adrenaline kicks in after a game, making me antsy, especially after a win. Thankfully, we don't have practice tomorrow. I'll be at the facility watching films for a few hours and working out, but I'll at least be able to sleep in.

It still feels like there's a wall growing between us that I want to smash before it grows larger.

I drop my bag and kick off my shoes, watching as Tessa heads to the fridge and pulls out a bottled water. She offers me one and I nod, meeting her there to take it from her.

"What's going on? And don't tell me nothing, or that you're tired. It's all bullshit, Tessa. I know you too well."

It's then I turn and on the counter is a small stack of pamphlets. I grab one, and it takes a minute to understand. "These yours?"

I flip through the rest. They're apartments. Some are nowhere near where I live but out in suburbs close to where Katie and Jude live. Others are closer to Debbie and Sawyer.

"What do you have these for?"

"Well if I stay, I need a place to live." She shuffles on her feet and as she reaches for her left ear, I reach out and take her hand, pushing it back down at the same time my hackles rise like a dog seeing a strange animal on its property.

I'll get back to the part where she hasn't considered staying here. With me.

"If?" My God. She still really hasn't decided yet. "I thought with the job..." I can't. I'm not sure I can handle this. She's been spending the last week working during the day, the night at my home games or with Debbie furiously planning their wedding. They went shopping over the weekend for baby cribs and other gear and she came back with bags of baby clothes for gifts for them. She hasn't spent a night outside my bed since the first night I brought her to it. And it's all still an *if?*

"Well..."

I give her time. Hard as it is. I wait a beat. Then two.

Three. When she still doesn't say anything I slap the pamphlets down on the counter. "Were you going to talk to me about it?"

"Stop." She flashes out her hand like a whip in the air. "You did this last time and felt like a dick afterward. Just give me a minute to gather my thoughts before you get pissy, all right?"

A muscle jumps in my jaw but I nod. She takes a large swill of her water before taking her sweet ass time twisting the top back on the bottle.

"I've been trying to talk to you about this, and I didn't know how because it seemed stupid and it's so soon and I still haven't fully decided anything."

My jaw grinds. It's hard to stay quiet, so I tilt my chin and bark out, "Okay."

"Jason." She laughs and comes near me. My back and shoulders brace for her touch before she places her palm at my chest. "You scare the shit out of me and it's not because you're looking at me right now like you want to tear me in two."

"I don't want to tear you into two. Maybe those apartment pamphlets, though."

"Well, see, I'm trying to figure out my future. And before you get all pissy, yes... of course it includes you, so drop your angry man act and *listen*."

Her hand slides up my chest, up my shoulder, down my arms. I ripped off the suit coat I have to wear to the arena as soon as we got into my truck but I don't miss the way her eyes heat as she draws her finger down my dress shirt.

"Tessa—" It's a warning but for the first time it lacks heat.

"Sorry, you're just so distracting."

"Apartments." I need to get us back on track before my brain travels south of my waist.

"Right. Well, if I stay, then I need a place to live, right?"

Shit. Has this been why she's been pulling away? I'm feeling like a dick again for being rude, but shit. She has a point and I haven't realized why this could be an issue for her until now.

"Will and you lived together and you're not all that hung up on moving in with me."

"Yeah," she says and frowns. And goddamn I want to kiss that worry of hers away but hell, I get it. I don't like it. But I get it.

I reach out slowly, because I'm still upset. All she had to do was talk to me about this. "Listen to me, Tessa. I told you at the beginning. You need time, I'll give it. You want to move in here? I want that. Straight up, no joke. I feel like I've waited a lifetime for you, and I don't want to lose you for any longer than I have to."

"Jason." Her lip trembles. "I don't even know if I'm staying yet."

"But you took the job with Sylvia."

"To see if I wanted it, I guess? Because I like the idea of being here. I do, and you're a huge part of that, but as crappy as my life in Toronto became, I'm not sure I'm ready to leave either. Not just to jump into bed with another guy."

I hate she says it like this. I hate she even thinks of me like *some guy*. I push that down. I've already been a jerk tonight, letting my own insecurity and worry of her walking away getting the better of me. Putting my own bullshit and wants and desires aside, I focus on her. Really focus on Tessa.

For as long as I've known her, she's been strong. Sure, I caught moments where she stumbled over her words and blushed when I was around. I knew she had her crush on me. But she's always been bold. And brave. And lately? I haven't seen that.

I don't know if Will did that to her, or if it's an effect of what happened only a few weeks ago, but ever since I started pushing her, she hasn't been the same spitfire she even was when I first saw her at Jude's a few weeks ago. She's been timid. Uncertain.

I hate I've had anything to do with that.

"Listen to me." I cup her cheek with my hand softly and wait for her gaze to meet mine. To really wait for her to focus. "I want you here. I want you with me. I get this might be crazy and too fast. I get we're still hiding a lot from people we love, but I want you to know, right now between the two of us, I want you *here*. Especially during the season when I'm going to be traveling so much. You'll have your space and time alone. Loads of it. It doesn't work out, we reevaluate. You want to set up your own home and have that, I get it and I'll try to be patient. Or... more so."

She chuckles and turns and then her lips are at my palm before tilting her face up to meet mine but I swear, that kiss on my palm... no woman has ever been so tender with me. "I shouldn't have hidden this from you, it's just that I talked to Antoine a couple days ago and I have to decide what I'm going to do. I only have a week of vacation left there available. And then you were gone and I started wondering if you wanted me here. Where would I live if you didn't? All that started racing and I didn't want to burden you at the beginning of the season."

"I get it. I do. Like I said, I'll try to be more understanding." And at the same time, figure out how to make her stay. I'm not ashamed of that. I want her here. In my home.

Always. "Come on. It's late. I'm fucking exhausted and we need some sleep."

"Sleep?"

As much as the disappointment in her tone makes me want to fuck her, I'm not kidding. Now, both my body and brain hurt. "Sleep." I pull her to me and kiss the top of her head. "Sleep. That's all. And I want you with me."

CHAPTER TWENTY-SEVEN

JASON

I WAKE up two mornings later to Tessa's alarm going off on her phone and her body pressed to mine. Two nights ago after we got back from the game, as soon as we got ready for bed and climbed in, she pressed her T-shirt covered chest to mine, wrapped her arm over my stomach and fell asleep almost immediately.

Last night was an entirely different story and we were awake well into the night. I couldn't get enough of her. She couldn't get enough of me and just when I thought we were done and completely spent, she pressed her thigh to me, arched her body, indicating she still wasn't done. So I fell asleep with the taste of her on my tongue and her breathless. And I am not complaining. I love sex with Tessa. She's not afraid to ask for what she wants. She's not afraid to let me take control and trust I'll give her everything she needs. I love her noises. Her body.

Hell, I just love her.

Inhaling the fruity scent of her shampoo, I can feel her short, little breaths across my bare chest. Every once in awhile through the night she shifted, burrowed closer to me and I slid my hand down her back, cupping her ass while she let out a sexy, breathy moan.

Even in her sleep she wants me. If she has to wait longer while she's awake to realize it, I'll be a man of my word and live up to the promises I made to her the other night.

But I'm done hiding my time spent with her. We've already had to do that after games when I wanted to wrap her in my arms. When we had dinner last weekend with Debbie and Sawyer.

Fucking Debbie and the comments she made the other night and the cute little wave, her wink, telling me she knows. I can only assume Tessa told her.

I doubt Sawyer does though since he hasn't tried taking me out at the shins with his stick yet, or anywhere else I value more than my legs, but that doesn't mean the possibility isn't there. He loves his sister. He also knows my reputation with women.

"Hey, sleepyhead." I tap Tessa's butt to wake her up. Her alarm is still singing some God-awful song.

"No." She presses her warm body closer to me. "No work. I'm on vacation."

I chuckle and kiss the top of her head. "Not today."

She groans unhappily and slowly twists her body, slapping the button on her phone. Silence descends before she curls back into me, eyes sleepy and barely open but her smile is sweet as sugar.

I barely have time to register her coming back to me before her lips are at the side of my throat and her body wedges itself against mine, one leg thrown over my thigh. Her leg brushes against my hard dick, hard from the morning, and sleeping so close to her all night long. Her center rubs against my hips and she hugs herself tight to me. This is exactly what she always does when she wants sex.

"Tessa," I warn. For the last week, we haven't spent time together in the morning. Yesterday, she slid out of bed and left for work without waking me up at all. I spent a few hours working out at the arena and then watching game films. Besides that, I've usually been up and already ready to head to the practice facility or out of town when she's had to get up in the morning. Today, we have a late morning skate, one of our last practices and finalizing lines before the season starts next week. "You need to get moving."

"Few more minutes." She sighs, presses the apex of her thighs harder against me and lets out a beautiful moan as she shivers and tenses.

Goddamn, this woman. She's perfect. "Few more minutes," I concede.

I roll her quickly to her back, surprising her with a little gasp. Then I take care of her with my fingers. Take care of both of us when I slide inside her tight, wet heat.

And later, when she's boneless, I carry her to the shower where I take care of her there too, but this time I do it hurrying her through the shower so she's not late for work.

"Have a good day," I say once we're in the kitchen. She's dressed in a killer pair of long black pants, wide legs that cup her ass perfectly and make her legs appear three times longer. Perhaps it's the heels peeking out from the bottom of them that give her the height. Whichever. Between the pants and a sexy pale pink top tucked in at the waist, she looks damn good.

And all mine.

I hand her a to-go cup of coffee I've already poured for

her and she leans in, kissing my cheek. "I'll see you tonight?"

"You bet your sweet ass you will. One more thing before you head out."

She slides her purse strap over her shoulder. "What is it?"

"I'm telling Sawyer. Today after practice."

I'm not sure I'm imagining it or not, but I swear her shoulders fall. With relief? Fear? "Okay. Good. No telling how long Debbie can keep that secret anyway. You'll let me know how it goes?"

I expect her to be concerned but thank God she's not. Maybe the conversation we had the other night finally helped her relax a bit.

All good things. But tonight, I have something better planned.

She needs more friends than Debbie. She needs a social life. She needs girls for wine nights and shopping sprees and spa days.

And luckily for me, I'm surrounded by damn good men with even better women who are full of fun times and craziness. So tonight's my Hail Mary, helping Tessa see how freaking good life can be if she decides to stay.

"Also, tonight, we're going out."

Hopefully, I can get the team to agree. Some might be hunkering down with their families before the wild travel schedule begins.

"Where?"

I know just the place. Tessa freaking loves to dance. "That's a surprise. But it'll be fun, that I promise."

She takes the few steps it takes to get to me and tilts her chin back. I bend down and kiss her, knowing what she's silently asking for. "I trust you."

My heart grows three sizes and I take the kiss deeper, risking her makeup and making her late for work if I don't control myself.

"Go," I growl against her mouth.

I'M TAKING my shot by risking interrupting Sawyer in his post-practice routine while most of the other guys have hit the showers. He's already taken one and I stand still for a moment while he meticulously rolls and folds each one of his socks individually before tucking them into the top right corner of his locker. Back in college, he had forgotten a pair of game socks in his bag and somehow, found an old hidden pair in his locker. They were folded the exact same way he's doing now. He had no idea who they belonged to and after freaking out that he wouldn't be able to play and Coach was going to kill him for not being prepared, he'd almost bawled like a damn baby when he found these socks. Now, they're not the exact same pair... but he still folds these massive large fuckers the same way.

For good luck and all because that game had been one of his best games ever and put him smack dab in the middle of being a first-round draft pick. It's been ten years and he still takes his superstitions seriously.

"Hey Sawyer," I call his name and leave space to prepare in case he lunges at me or throws a punch. Not gonna lie, I'm not sure how he's never caught on to my interests in Tessa considering it's been me for the last several years reminding him to call her or send her a gift on her birthday, but I'll be shocked as hell if he suspects anything.

"What's up?" He has his head dipped down, meticulously rolling a damn sock. I've always given him shit for being so particular but no way am I touching it now.

"Thought tonight, we'd get the team together. And the women and head to Roxbury's."

He twists his neck and looks up at me from his spot on the bench. "*You* want to go to the eighties and nineties dance club?"

Yeah, I can see how this would be a surprise to him.

"Thought Tessa could use a night to dance. Get to know some of the women more."

"So send the women."

"Right. Let me call 'em all up and demand they take out your little sister to a club."

His dark brows burrow together. And finally, finally he stops with the sock bullshit. "What's going on?"

"She hasn't decided if she's staying here yet. Thought maybe a night out having some fun could help that choice along."

"She might leave?" He jolts from his spot on the bench and I step back. Around us, some of the first and second lines are getting done with their showers and the noise picks up. Classic locker room bullshit. I drown it all out and focus on Sawyer. "She can't. I'm having a baby. She has to stay. Fuck, she doesn't have anything left to return to."

"Which is why I want her to feel connected to more than just you and Debbie. Or me."

"Yeah. Yeah. Of course, I get it." He runs his hand through his hair and blows out a breath. "She's still that uncertain? I figured when she took the job—"

"Me too." I shouldn't have assumed. If I'd asked more questions, none of the other night would have happened. "Listen, there's something else—"

"Will?" His jaw goes so tight I'm surprised it doesn't shatter.

"No. I need to tell you something and you gotta promise not to get pissed."

"I don't make those promises. You start with that, I guarantee I'm going to get pissed."

I can go with the slow and easy route, but instead I decide to rip it off like a band-aid. If he punches me, I'd rather not draw it out. "Tessa and me. We're together."

"Yeah, living together."

"Right. In a way, I don't want her to ever leave."

"Well, yeah, I don't want her to leave either."

Swear to God this guy was dropped on his head multiple times as a baby. Many multiple times. My best friend is not the sharpest crayon in the box.

"Sawyer, man." I shake my head and try not to laugh. "I *like* your sister. Tessa. In a way that means we're not living together as roommates, but we're dating. Like dating dating."

There's a pause. Maybe twelve. I have no idea how many beats of my heart pass while Sawyer gapes at me, either clueless still or processing.

"If you hurt her I'll kill you," he finally says.

"That's it?"

"You want me to what, fuck you up? Be pissed?"

I mean, I don't *want* that, but I sort of figured it'd be the natural progression of things.

Now it's my turn to stare at him, stupefied. He huffs a laugh and shakes his head before taking his seat back on the bench.

"You're my best friend, the best man I've ever met and you've known her for years. You know what she needs. Why would I be pissed if you two finally started dating?"

Maybe because I'm also sleeping with his sister. I'm not sure he's gotten that far yet.

"You serious about this? Because I've been hesitant as hell to have this conversation with you and if you're just playing along so you can kick my ass when I'm not expecting it, I'd rather get that over with right now."

"You care about her?"

"Yes." I love her, but I'm not telling him before I tell her.

"She's not just one of the women you fuck and dump?"

"No. Fuck. Of course not. It's Tessa."

"See. That right there. You look like now I'm going to be the one getting a fist to my face because I only implied that. So why would I be pissed when I know you'll take care of her?"

He has a point. Also, it takes effort to relax the fists I've made.

This has gone... well, shit... this has not gone the way I assumed it would at all. I stare at Sawyer for another beat and then grin. "Getting married and becoming a dad has made you soft."

"Fuck off." He glares at me and this time, I know he's going to do it. "Fuck off, J. I'm not soft."

"You're so damn soft you could be one of those biscuits your mom makes." Damn, those things are good. Soft and gooey on the inside.

This time he lunges and I'm prepared. I let him take me to the floor and we roll around like idiots, laughing, getting slapped in the asses and back and head with towels from the other guys on the team as they join in our insanity.

When we're done, Sawyer's pinned in front of me, his arm pulled back into an armbar. "Who's soft, Chauncy?"

"Fuck off, asshole."

"We'll see you tonight at the Roxbury?"

"Yes. You fool. Now get off me."

I let him go, giving him a playful shove that sends him almost to his knees.

"You're a dick."

"Yup."

"I love you like a brother."

"Someday I could be one."

"Yeah... that'd be pretty fucking awesome, too."

I reach forward and slap his chest. I need to get home to see Tessa before tonight but I want to get her a few things beforehand.

"Later."

"I'm serious about killing you if you fuck up," he calls out as I'm walking away.

I throw my hand in the air in acknowledgment. I've already screwed this up along the way. I'm determined not to let it happen again.

CHAPTER TWENTY-EIGHT

Tessa

MY HANDS ARE clasped together behind Jason's neck. I figured the guy could dance with the way he can move his hips in bed, the man can *move*. We've been out on the dance floor so long he has sweat at his temples and sideburns.

So. Damn. Sexy.

And his ability to grind his hips, making me think of sex while I'm in the heels he once told me he wanted me wearing and nothing else? I'm about ready to pack this night in and spend some time with him dancing horizontally.

I would, but I'm having a freaking blast.

"Have I thanked you yet for bringing me out?" I kiss his sweaty cheek and smile up at him.

His hands at my back press me closer, as if I can get closer. "Only a dozen times."

"Well, I really mean it this time."

"Good." He twists his head to the side, we've had to shout in each other's ears to be heard and kisses me. His tongue slides across my seam and I open for him. He's cool despite the heat pouring off him and tastes like fresh water since that's all he's been drinking all night.

Me, on the other hand? I'm a few glasses of wine in and having the time of my life.

When he came back to his place earlier and told me to dress to dance, I'd looked at him strangely.

"What? Why?"

"Because you've had weeks of stress. Months and years of it if I'm guessing and you don't get out enough. We're going to shake off your funk and let you have some fun."

"We?"

"Talked to Sawyer."

"And since you don't have a black eye, I'm assuming it went well?" In all honesty, I hadn't been all that worried. I figured Sawyer would call me and warn me. Or Jason would have called if something went wrong but I hadn't lied to Jason that morning. I trust him. It's that simple.

"Told me his best guy with his favorite sister was pretty damn cool. Wouldn't want it any other way. Said if he can't trust me with you, who can he trust?"

"Really?" I sway toward the counter, catching myself. *"He said that?"*

"Basically." He shrugged and came near me, one hand immediately going to the back of my neck, the other to my waist where he bent to kiss me. *"Now, get dressed to dance. We're going to Roxbury's."*

"The nineties club?" I've been there before. It's a freaking blast. You see people dressed in their favorite eighties and nineties pop and rock characters, moms in their forties reliving their glory days. Plus, the music freaking rocks.

And Jason knows how much I love it.

"Yeah. Go and get dressed. We'll go somewhere for a good meal first. And wear the heels."

A shiver rolls down my spine. I have something incredibly sexy to look forward to later.

And now we're here, and I was absolutely right. I've barely left the dance floor. I've danced with Debbie and Byron Maddox's wife, Hannah. I've danced with Katie. With Regan, Duke Fletcher's, wife.

But through it all, Jason has been here. Close by, spinning me out with a quick flick of his wrist and twirling me back in. Moving his hips. Rocking out with me and the girls while most of the guys stay upstairs in the private VIP area he reserved for the night.

I can't remember the last time I've had so much fun or hung out with so many incredible women. They're all *awesome.*

"I like this," I say. "But I think I need a break." My feet are getting sore in the heels. My ankles are on fire and even though I spend an hour running several times a week, my thighs are trembling.

"Let's get you a drink and a break then," Jason says. He smiles down at me and he's blindingly beautiful. Possibly more so since I've practically moved into his bed. If Jason made me dizzy before the last couple weeks, there's no explaining the way I feel around him now. Even when he gets impatient.

We can't all be perfect. But I can see him trying, and that's all I want.

"Come on, then." He grabs my hand and pulls me off the dance floor. We're near the bottom of the stairs that will take us to the VIP area when his eyes narrow and he focuses on something. I try to see what he sees but there's so many people.

"What the hell?"

"What?"

"I think that's Paisley."

He points to a pretty little thing near the bar, stumbling off the dance floor. He's right. I've only met her a couple times, but she's super cute. And sweet. "Didn't you say she and Mikah were coming?"

"Yeah, but he's not here yet. I'd know." He frowns at her and then looks down at me. "Go upstairs. I'm going to talk to her. Maybe they snuck in while we were on the floor."

"You sure?"

"Yeah. I'll be right up."

"All right." He kisses me and taps my butt. I wobble up the stairs, grimacing at how quickly my feet are starting to kill. I should know better. New heels need to be broken in before you spend hours on them. Plus, I haven't exactly been wearing a whole lot of dress shoes in the last few weeks. I thank the bouncer at the top who's blocked off our area and slide into a booth next to Debbie.

She danced for the first hour or so before claiming she was too tired to do more, so she's been up here most of the night, sipping water and lemonade, probably wanting to go home but refusing until I'm ready. Apparently she offered to drive Jason and me back home to his place tonight. As for my brother, he's been *hovering* and I can understand why she's getting irritated with him.

"My legs freaking kill," I groan. I bend down and unknot the tie at the back of my ankle and slide my feet loose. I'm careful to keep my shoes on but my squished toes need some serious breathing room.

Debbie laughs and pokes me in the ribs. "You having fun?"

"God yes. I needed this. I can't remember... I can't remember when I've had this much fun."

Possibly the last time I came down here and we did this.

"Jason planned this for you," she says, and while I'm not completely surprised, it still startles me.

"Yeah?"

"Told Sawyer he wanted you to get to know the girls." She nods across the table where Katie and Hannah are gabbing, Hannah almost falling off her chair she's laughing so loud. I laugh with her. At her. I don't even know what's so funny but Hannah is hilarious. "Thought maybe it'd help your decision."

"Hmmm." I refill my wineglass from the bottle on the table. I'm not exactly sure I like he planned this to manipulate me, but did he? Maybe he really wants me to see all I can have here. And honestly, I can't find a single thing wrong with this crew or this life.

Damn.

As I settle into what I'm realizing, Jason storms up the stairs, Paisley's hand in his. He pulls her over to Jude and I'm sliding out of the booth. He looks pissed and even next to me I hear Debbie mutter a, "oh shit, what's wrong?"

"I'll let you know," I say and I go to stand by Sawyer who's already felt the mood change as well.

She's sandwiched by Katie and then surrounded by Jude. I'm on the other side of the huddle as Jason pulls them all over. "Mikah broke up with her," he says.

My jaw falls. I can't believe this. There's a whole lot of talking. A whole lot of Paisley protesting they don't do anything. A whole lot more of the guys arguing with her before the guys' decision echoes through all of it.

"Let's go," Jason says. His hand has at some point settled on my lower back and I feel him tug on me. "I'll be back, okay? Or have Debbie take you to my place whenever you want to leave."

"What's going on?"

"I don't know, but we'll figure it out. Mikah wouldn't end it if something hadn't happened. He likes her too much. Plus, he loves her with Angelo."

"What are you going to do?"

"Talk to Mikah. Knock some sense into his ass."

He looks ready to rumble. "Be careful," I say. I haven't hidden my affection for him tonight.

Sawyer gagged a few times until Debbie elbowed him earlier, but I've at least tried to keep it to the dance floor. But now? With Jason ready to fight for a friend of his who he thinks is making a bad decision, or at least a fucked up one? I can't hold back.

"Hurry home," I tell him in his ear after I kiss him, "so I'm awake with nothing but the heels on or you're going to miss out huge."

He slams his mouth to mine, digs his fingers into my hair and then pulls back, dark eyes *burning*. "Deal. Go take care of Paisley. She can use some friends."

In the midst of all of this her other two friends have already joined our group, one model-beautiful girl looking at all the guys on the team like they're naked.

I feel this deeply in my soul. Heading back to my spot, I grab my wine and take a healthy sip, watching Jason and Jude and Klaus hurry to figure out what happened with Mikah.

Paisley sits and explains what happened while I keep my eyes on the stairs where Jason disappeared, thinking of the concern on his face. At the fact a friend and teammate of his could be in trouble? He wasted no time in going after him to make sure things are okay.

Because that's the kind of guy Jason is.

He's the best guy I've ever met, despite our screw ups and his impatience. But when he cares about someone, he never once hesitates to let them know. Or do what he can do to protect them.

I've been pushing him away for no reason. Absolutely no reason at all, except for my own silly fears, which are completely unfounded.

Which means there's only one decision to make.

I drain the rest of my glass of wine and pour a fresh one. Then I tilt my head and press it on Debbie's shoulder. "I'm going to call Antoine in the morning and put in my notice in Toronto and I'm moving here."

"I always knew you would," she says, wrapping her arm around my back and hugging me to her side. "But I'm super super happy to hear it."

"Super duper happy? Not just happy? Or super happy?"

"Super duper, and don't tease me. I'm working on not swearing in front of the baby."

Her hand goes to her belly. I throw my head back and laugh.

Then we spend the night dancing and when it's late, Debbie's exhausted, and my feet can't take another minute crammed into the heels, she and Sawyer drop me off at Jason's building where I wait another couple hours for him to come home.

WHEN JASON ARRIVES, I'm sitting on the couch. Tired. Still slightly drunk while trying not to fall asleep and drinking water to help keep me awake.

He opens the door, flips on the light, sees me, and his keys fall to the floor.

I'm not surprised by his reaction but a thrill of excitement pulses through my blood.

After all, I've been waiting for him in nothing but the sexy heels he requested and an even sexier, lacy lingerie set I picked up a few days ago when I went shopping for more work attire.

"You're late," I say, standing, walking toward him so he can see the full effect of everything I'm wearing and everything I'm *not*. The negligee barely covers my sex and the cool air in his apartment as I walk toward him does little to stop the heat traveling through me.

"And you're a fucking vision."

"Everything go okay with Mikah?"

He reaches for me, runs his hand down my arm. Just a fingertip. It's enough to ignite the embers that have been smoldering since I put this tiny little thing on.

"He is *not* what we're going to talk about right now."

"Oh?" I tilt my head to the side. "What do you want to talk about then?"

Jason's eyes are on my breasts and he licks his lips before dragging his heated, smoldering gaze up to me. "I don't want any talking at all."

He closes the space between us and wraps his arm around my lower back, yanking me to him in one solid, fluid movement. I go easily like I'm floating on air.

Right before his head comes down and our lips brush, I whisper, "Not even if it's to hear that I'm staying? Moving here—"

I get nothing else out because his mouth slams to mine and he steals the rest of my words with a kiss that heats me to my toes. I'm lifted into the air as he kisses me, him grunting as I dig my heels into his back.

Something tells me by the bulge already pressing against me that he *likes* it when I hurt him and he likes it a whole lot.

I expect him to carry me down the hall like he's done so many times already but instead, he walks me straight to his couch and tosses me down.

"Hey!" I bounced on his cushions and his hand presses to my stomach. "Don't fucking move an inch."

Well, alright then. I stay exactly how I landed, legs spread, one foot on the floor and my arms above my head while he rips off his shirt and shoves down his shorts. He grabs his wallet before he tosses the shorts to the floor, flips open his billfold and he has a condom in his hand when he flicks his wallet over his shoulder.

His underwear comes next and my mouth waters as he takes himself in hand, strokes his wide, hard length while he inspects every single inch of me with his gaze.

Good Lord, the man is so unbelievably hot I should be slapping myself for doubting him, or this, or us for a single second. I'd tell him that if I could form words but soon he's sheathed himself, dropped to his knees, and yanked my hips toward his waiting mouth where I lose all rational thought, all words except for *please, more, harder,* and his name and maybe God's as he takes me to heights unknown with orgasms that leave me listless.

CHAPTER TWENTY-NINE

JASON

SHE'S STAYING.

We didn't talk about it all last night, but mostly because I saw her in the sexy little getup and completely lost all interest in any conversation that didn't involve me telling her where to put her legs, her mouth, or how fast to ride me. Which she did once I took care of us on the couch before carrying her to my room where we did it again.

Last night, after I left the club, the guys and I went to talk some sense into Mikah. When he told us about his baby's mother, Angela, coming back into the picture and threatening to take him away or make life extra difficult for Mikah and Angelo, we then took off to other clubs to try to find Angela and the puck bunnies she used to party with.

Unfortunately, none of them had seen her, but it took longer than I expected.

I also expected Tessa to be asleep in my bed when I

returned since it was so late. Thankfully she continues to be full of surprises of the absolute sexiest kind imaginable.

I still haven't had the chance to fuck her in only those heels of hers, but the outfit she had on more than makes up for it.

Now it's morning, she's snoring softly next to me, tangled in my sheets and blanket with one of her legs draped over mine like she always tends to do. We don't always cuddle, and sometimes I get too damn hot if she presses her body next to mine, but always, every night since she started sleeping in my bed, I've woken up with her connected to me somehow.

And I love the feeling of her thigh as I run my hand down it, watching her sleep, listening to the quiet sounds she makes as she does. Sometimes she mumbles, throws out a few random words. Even in her sleep, Tessa is full of life and sass and I send up a quiet plea that now that she's finally agreed to move here, I'll never see that spark dim from her again.

Today, we have talking to do. Plans to make. I have to head to the gym for a workout at some point, but mostly I want to spend the day with Tessa. A regular Saturday with no games and no practices where we can be *us* outside the game.

Sliding gently out of bed so I don't wake her, I cover her with the comforter to keep her warm before I head to the bathroom where I do a quick clean-up and teeth brush. Then, I head to the kitchen, pull up a food delivery app and schedule a breakfast delivery from a local restaurant called Stack's that has the best sausage I've ever tasted. I throw in a couple extra sides of bacon for Tessa and set about making coffee.

A part of me wants to go take a shower and get cleaned

up, but I also want to take that shower with Tessa and since we were up long into the morning, the right thing to do is let her sleep. Fortunately, she doesn't enjoy sleeping in, similar to me, so I'm on my second cup of coffee when she comes stumbling into the kitchen, phone in her hand and wearing one of my dress shirts, buttoned halfway and crookedly.

I grin over the edge of my coffee cup as she heads straight toward the coffee. Once she's poured herself a cup and dumped her favorite caramel flavored creamer in it I left out for her.

It's only then she turns to me, grins, and takes her first sip. "Good morning."

I push back in my chair away from the table where I've been scrolling through the news and hold out my arm. "Come here, sweetheart."

She does, bare feet pad toward me until she settles herself on my lap, curling into me.

"See you found my side of the closet," I tease her, tugging at the collar.

"It was too far to my room to get dressed."

The thought to tell her to move her stuff into my room comes to my lips but I hold back. She needs time. She might not move in with me permanently.

"It looks good on you." I kiss her temple and hold her close while she drinks her coffee, blowing gently over the rim to cool it off. "I ordered breakfast. Should be here any minute."

"Thank you." Her head falls to my shoulder and she sets her coffee down. I have one hand on her hip and the other wrapped around her back. We sit like this quietly for a few minutes, and I have to say, Tessa curled into me in a chair might even be more enjoyable than having sex with her on my couch. It means she trusts me. Wants this. *Me.*

Finally.

"We should talk about what you said last night."

"You mean the sentence you didn't let me finish?"

"Yeah, but I think you enjoyed the way we ended that conversation."

Her body shakes as she laughs and I kiss her temple again. I can't *not* kiss her and thankfully, she doesn't seem to mind at all.

"Yes, I enjoyed that," she says, still laughing. "In fact, I think we should end more conversations in the same way."

I am in definite agreement with her. "Anytime you want it, all you got to do is ask."

Her laughter freezes and she jolts. It's minimal, but enough I frown and pull back so I can see her face. When I do, I see her eyes glazed over in thought, an expression I know on her face very well by now. She's turned on.

"What is it?" I jostle her until she shakes her head.

"Nothing. I was thinking. Well, remembering."

She sips her coffee but the mug in her hand trembles back and forth. I take it from her and turn her so she has to look at me.

"What were you remembering, Tessa?" Her cheeks have deepened in color and my interest is piqued.

She laughs. "It's silly. But a dream I had one day."

Ah. Now we're getting somewhere fun. "A sex dream?"

She nibbles the bottom corner of her lip and shrugs. "Yeah. I woke up to my alarm blaring *anyway you want it,* so what you said made me remember it."

"Tell me it was of me." She'd mentioned fantasizing about me before. She also said she wouldn't tell me what they were. But no way am I *not* pushing this one.

She grins up at me, presses her soft but warm hand to

my cheek and leans up, brushing her lips over mine. "It was a recurring dream. One where you took my virginity."

And... I'm hard. My dick is pressed against her hip and I know she feels it. I also know she sees it when she looks down at me and smirks. I'm about to demand she tells me everything about this dream when my phone dings with an alert saying breakfast is here.

"Saved by the bell," I tell her, gently sliding her off my lap. "Our breakfast is here, but later... we're going to continue this conversation."

"Yes sir," she says, mock serious with the worst salute I've ever seen.

Goddamn, I love this woman.

I answer my phone and text down to the front lobby that they can send up the delivery and wait by the opened door for the elevator to open. I get a wide-eyed look from the middle-aged man delivering me my food but I'd forgotten I was only in my underwear. I don't know if he recognizes me or if he's stunned by the fact my dick is still semi-hard. Oh well.

When I return to the kitchen with a bag filled with food, Tessa has wrapped her hair into what looks like a bird's nest on top of her head and she's on her laptop, sipping her coffee.

"What's up?" I ask, placing the containers on the table before I turn and grab silverware. "And do you need a refresh?"

"Please." She pushes away her coffee mug and closes her laptop. "And I was drafting my resignation letter."

I try to minimize the excitement this causes me as I pull out the silverware and pick up her coffee. As I'm refilling it, she says, "Yeah. I figure I can call Antoine today. It's a Saturday, but he won't mind me calling him at home, but I'd at least like to give him a heads-up. Then I can officially submit my resignation on Monday. Since I already have a job, I plan on giving him two weeks but I doubt he'll make me come back and work given the circumstances so I guess... that's done." She chews on her lip for a moment before continuing. I slide her fresh cup to her and take the seat across from her. "Then there's my apartment. My lease isn't up until the end of the year, so I might have to pay a fee."

"I'll cover it."

"No." She shakes her head but I stop her.

"Pay me back if you want, but let me make this easier for you. You don't have the money for two month's rent, do you?"

Her face curls up into something happy but she eventually shakes her head. The nest of her hair on top wobbles to and fro. "No. I don't. And thanks. I'll pay you back."

I've offered because I have the money, but no way in hell will I take her money. Unless she insists when the time comes, but then I'll just spend it on her anyway so I let it go. I have millions. A few thousand dollars to break a lease is pocket change.

"You okay with all of this?" I dig into the bag and pull out the containers. As I do, Tessa moans happily when she sees the massive pile of bacon. This girl. I love her excitement for food. It's almost as sexy as the sounds she makes when she comes.

"Yeah. Guess it feels weird, not returning. Like I don't know... like I'm not getting closure?" She chomps on a piece of bacon and focuses on me. "Does that sound weird?"

Kind of, but I doubt she's really asking for my opinion but more thinking out loud. I reach across the table and take her hand in mine. "What can I do to make it better for you?"

She sets down her bacon and picks up my hand covering her other one, kissing my palm. Then my wrist. Never once does she take her shimmering blue eyes off me and eventually she smiles. "I think... I think all I need is you."

CHAPTER THIRTY

Tessa

IT IS FREAKING *cold* as the winter air whips through the streets. I have definitely not missed this kind of weather and even for early November in Chicago, this seems brutally cold. The local news said they're in an unseasonably cold snap. All I know is that the North Face puffer coat I bought a couple weeks ago especially for this trip and the scarf wrapped around my neck are doing very little to protect me from the biting chill. It was still ninety in Charlotte last week and I spent most of one of my days off lounging in the pool and Katie and Jude's house.

Currently, my teeth are chatting as I do my job, standing on the sidewalk as the guys from the Ice Kings step out of the bus and grab their luggage. It's one of the most mundane parts of this job, but sometimes herding a professional hockey team is much like what I imagine it is to manage a group of kindergartners.

We're here for three days for two back-to-back games

against the Chicago Storm team before heading up to Buffalo and then Toronto. It's the beginning of a weeklong travel schedule, the longest I've done yet and while I'm not at all excited to head back to Toronto, I am excited to see my parents who will have seats next to me at the game, courtesy of Jason.

Next to me, Katie has traveled this leg of the trip with the team so she can come back to her old stomping grounds, see Jude play against one of his best friends and Storm goalie, Garrett Dubiak. She also is excited to see her old co-workers who will be at tonight's game with her and her best friend, Lizzie.

"I never imagined how crazy their travel really is. And I'm impressed, you have this down to a science already."

"I've been getting a lot of practice." Seven away games in the last five weeks since the regular season has started. Sylvia has had me traveling with her to most of them, doing more than she usually does but she wants to know I can manage it without her at some point. Which means her eagle eyes hidden behind the glasses are never far from me. Even now I can feel her boring into me, making sure I don't screw up. Thankfully, it's happened infrequently.

My job is incredible. Never boring. I'm always on the move and there's always some sort of fire to put out or a schedule to change. Minor injuries mean guys who would travel stay home and someone gets called up from the bench meaning flight manifests need changing. Rooms need rearranging. There was the trip to Anaheim a few weeks ago where somehow half of the gear wasn't unloaded from the team plane and half the team was in the locker room waiting for the gear to arrive up until warm-ups started instead of hours earlier like it should have.

That did not make Sylvia happy. Fortunately, she didn't blame me.

Katie might see me with my iPad that I can't live without, checking to make sure all the guys disembark from the bus we brought from the airplane to the hotel, and they're all grabbing their right luggage items beneath, but this is the easy part.

The hard part is herding them all to the stadiums after a night of partying on the road wins even if all the drinking they do is just in the hotel lobby.

Some of these guys can get monstrously grouchy when hungover.

Plus, I'm usually tired and not in the mood for them mostly because Jason and I do our own celebrating... in my own travel room... late into the night.

No, the hardest part is coordinating the deliveries of gear, ensuring everyone who is traveling has their name on the flight manifest on the team's private plane. It's double-checking and confirming the reservations for the hotels because more than once those have been missing and it was a race to get a new block scheduled close enough to the venues where they'd play, not so close they'd be hounded or found by fans.

I never realized so much went into all their travel either, and frankly, I'm learning none of the guys on the team pay much attention. Jason himself has been surprised when I come home exhausted and worn out from dealing with parts of my job, but all of it has been absolutely thrilling.

I don't miss Toronto or my job. I haven't given Will a single thought since I made the decision to stay. Instead, my life has become surrounded by friends, both wives and girlfriends of the players, my co-workers at the team's headquarters, and even a book club I joined but have only been able to attend one meeting. Still, the women were incredibly fun and we did more dishing about life over a few bottles of wine than the latest fiction book we were supposed to read.

Essentially, there's nothing I'm missing and sometimes I pinch myself because I'm so damn happy.

As Jason once promised me, we fight. A lot. We bicker over who leaves more dirty clothes all over the condo (unfortunately, that's me), who leaves more dirty dishes in the sink (definitely him). We bicker over whose car to drive when we go out on dates. I've recently bought a brand new Jeep Wrangler truck I freaking adore, but Jason always insists on driving his Escalade.

We fight over what to eat for dinner, whether or not I'm cooking... which... nope. Not after a day at work. We argue over whether to stay in for a night or head to George's Bar with his teammates. Which honestly, is my favorite place to go. We show up and it's like one huge boisterous family and even often includes the other customers joining in on the fun in a way that still says the guys can be themselves. I've joined Jason for a few marketing events and fundraising dinners.

We are *busy*. And I love every minute of it.

And him.

Plus, I'm in full swing helping Debbie plan her wedding which is going surprisingly easy, mostly because she's so laid back. The only thing she keeps worrying about is her dress fitting when the day comes because now, at almost twenty weeks, her tummy seems to grow every time I see her.

Oh... and the nursery has now been painted a dark navy blue and is fully decorated for the boy they're having. Just thinking about their baby brings tears to my eyes. Along with how I ever could have thought of leaving them during all of this.

Or Jason. We might fight a lot, but we also laugh more than I ever thought humanly possible.

We also have more sex than I ever could have imagined. And it's not just good sex. It's incredible sex. Always. Every single time he ensures he finishes me off at least once and my abs have never been tighter. My stamina has never been better and I'm not even getting the opportunity to run as much as I want. It's him.

Speaking of, Katie nudges me in the waist with her elbow, hard enough to poke through my thick and fluffy coat. "Hotties at three o'clock."

I snort, but I still watch Jason and Jude stumble off the bus, shoving each other playfully and laughing. They both have a pair of headphones draped around their necks and fancy wool pea coats on over their suits.

"Damn. They are so freaking hot," I mutter.

This time, Katie laughs. I've become closer to her more than any other girlfriend outside Debbie, mostly because we spend a lot of time at their house in the suburbs. So much so that when a house in their neighborhood came on the market a couple of weeks ago Jason asked me to go look at it with him. I'd hesitated, but only because the thing was so big and I like our condo and easy life. He didn't end up making an offer, but I think that was only because I was uncertain.

Since then, he's talked about us getting a house together. Moving somewhere bigger. He's pushing me gently but I know where he's leading.

To us—starting a family together. And it's not that I'm opposed, it's just that I like things how they are right now and I want to enjoy them.

"Hey handsome," I say through my chattering teeth, rolling to my toes to kiss him.

"You're as cold as ice," he says, smiling against my cold teeth.

"I suppose you'll have to warm me up then."

"After the game, I'm all yours."

They only have a few hours to rest and unwind at the hotel before we head over to the Storm's arena. Until then, I have to make sure all the guys get their room keys and get to where they need to be. I'll head over early with Sylvia so this will be the last time I see Jason until he takes the ice.

Which is always a sexy sight to behold.

"Play hard and good luck."

"Please," Jude scoffs, Katie wrapped in his arms and shivering almost as much as me. "We don't need luck when we're the best."

I roll my eyes. Their confidence has no limits. But it's also warranted. The Ice Kings have taken an early lead in their division this season and they're already up three games in the first place spot.

"You watching with our parents tonight?" Jude asks.

I've already confirmed, double-checked, and triple-checked their tickets. "Yup. I'll be in the box with them, Katie, and Lizzie and... Noah?" I ask, turning to Katie. I think that's the name of her co-worker she invited.

"Yep. He's bringing his boys. Should be a blast."

"Only if Dad doesn't threaten to roast a goat when he doesn't like a call."

I throw my head back and laugh. John Sr. is hilarious and has the most colorful cursing language I've ever witnessed. For some strange reason, it usually involves farm animals. I'm not certain what he has against them, but I've almost peed myself laughing at him more than once in the few games they've come to.

His mom Sonya is adorable. Sweet and classy but her innuendo knows no bounds.

I love Jason's entire family and I can't wait to spend Thanksgiving with them. They're all headed down to Charlotte. Joey has a game the next night in Tennessee so he can make it and because of Sawyer and Debbie's wedding plans means Jason won't be with his family then, Jude and Katie offered to host.

"All right, boys." I clap my hands and shoo them inside. "Go get your rooms. We'll see you later, okay?"

"Yes, ma'am." Jude salutes me, kisses Katie and pulls her along with him.

Jason leans down and gives me my own kiss on still frozen lips that quickly warm under his tender but persistent kiss. "Love you, Tessa," he murmurs, pulling back.

My jaw drops and I'm speechless. He's never said that to me. Not like this. I've heard a lot of *I love the way you sleep. I love fucking you. I love your blue eyes. I love your damn sexy shoes.* When it comes to Jason, he's liberal with things he loves about me or us, but he's ever once said he loves *me.*

I can't even come up with a response because by the time I will my mouth to remember how to work, he's already walking through the hotel revolving doors, tugging his headphones back over his ears.

He didn't even look back at me!

The jerk. He didn't wait for me to say it back.

LOVE YOU, Tessa.

Love you, Tessa.

I have no idea how I've gotten any work done since Jason walked away from me. And then, it seems he avoided me once I finally was able to get into the hotel to settle in my room. I tried texting him, asking to see him, and he never responded. It's like he wants me freaking out!

Now, we're in the third period of the Chicago game. Lizzie and Katie are both on their feet with ten minutes to go and the game tied at three. Lizzie's wearing a Storm jersey, Katie is in Jude's and they've been playfully bickering back and forth all game over who has the better goalie.

Maddox is, obviously.

Lizzie is adamant it's Garrett Dubiak. I do have to admit, he's playing one hell of a game, stopping everything Jason flung at him so far. The goals have come from Lutzgo and Jude and I can almost feel Jason's frustration from way up in the box.

John Sr.'s frustration for his son is equally palpable, but that's just because he keeps screaming.

"Yes! Take that chicken feeder!" he yells at one of Chicago's defenseman who Jason skates by, dribbling his puck before releasing it to Lutzgo, he doesn't get a shot before he's lodged into the corner against two of Chicago's players and they come out with the puck, slapping it away from the goal.

"Freaking holy roosters. Score, damn it."

I could sit through every single game next to John and never grow bored. The man is crazy... also, crazy handsome. All of the Taylor boys look so similar to their dad in build and height and muscle mass but get their darker coloring from Sonya. Jason, though, is the only one with John's dark eyes. It's like seeing what Jason will look like in twenty or thirty years, and the view is not disappointing.

Unfortunately, I need to be downstairs and in the hallways before the game ends to ensure everyone gets to where they're supposed to be on time. Fortunately, I don't have to stick around to make sure the crates of gear are loaded for our flight out since we have two more nights in Chicago. There have been a few away trips where I don't make it back to the hotel until hours after Jason and the rest of the team, it can take so long to get everything loaded and checked.

"I need to head out," I say, kissing John Sr. on the cheek and hugging Sonya. They've made it clear they're huggers, and give their affection freely. "You take care and we'll see you soon?"

"Yeah, yeah," John mutters, waving me off. He's already focused on the game. "Damn cheatin' cheetahs out there is what they all are."

I snort, pushing his animalistic curses out of my mind and say goodbye to the rest of those with us and hugging Katie. "See you tomorrow?"

"Wouldn't miss it," she says.

We have plans to do some serious damage to the stores on Michigan Avenue.

I'm back downstairs when the final buzzer goes off and Carolina takes the win with a goal scored in the final two minutes by Jason. Finally.

That'll put him in a good mood. Although, I'm hoping what I have to tell him makes him smile just as much.

I'M IN SHOES. New shoes with a bright red heel and nothing else, propped against the large writing desk in the hotel room before he returns. It's a replay of the night at the bar, except this time, my heels are more conservative and I forgot to pack the negligée. The heels and the length of my hair covering my breasts with already hardened nipples are my only accessories, but this time, I'm no longer nervous as I hear Jason use his key card to enter the room.

I'm off to the side and around the corner so he can't see me when he enters, but I stay quiet as he heads to the bathroom, flipping on lights and almost blinding me with it.

The bathroom door opens and he calls my name.

"Over here," I say quietly.

I love the way he looks at me, the way I can surprise him. The way his jaw drops and his dark eyes heat as he takes me in.

He rips at his tie, loosening it before throwing it on the bed. "What's this greeting for?"

He shrugs out of his suit coat, tears at buttons on his shirt which is sort of a bummer. I enjoy undressing him.

His belt comes next, the whistling sounds makes me shiver as he yanks it through his belt loops and takes a step closer to me.

I've completely forgotten what I was going to say to him.

He stops moving when his hands go to his button at his pants and calls my name.

"Yes?" I'm staring at his quickly growing bulge. Looks mighty uncomfortable behind those tight pants. Perhaps I should kiss it and make it all better. I lick my lips to wet them.

"What's with the greeting, not that I'm complaining."

Oh. Right. I have something to say.

I reluctantly take my eyes off his groin, drag them up the bricks of his abdomen, the ridges of his pecs and the muscles at his shoulder to see him swallow thickly, his jaw jutted, before reaching his eyes.

"I love you, too," I say.

His smile shakes before popping through. "I thought that might have freaked you out."

"It didn't. I want to hear it again. Every day."

"Then that's what you'll get." He undoes his pants and shoves them down to the floor, tugging off his socks and underwear.

My hands curl around the edge of the desk as he makes his way to me, stroking himself, looking like a vicious warrior and a seductive beast all in one.

"Turn around," he commands, stopping just out of my reach.

"I thought..."

"I'll tell you I love you again when I'm deep inside of you, you're ready to come and screaming it back."

Oh. Well then. Who am I to argue with that plan?

I do as he says and inhale a sharp breath when he reaches around to my front, fingers finding my slickness and his teeth are at my shoulder. "Wet. Always so wet."

"For you. Always."

"Good."

He plays with me, fingers moving exactly how I like them and then he slams inside of me. The sting of my body accepting him and accommodating his size even after all these weeks still takes me a second to adjust to, but as soon as I nod I'm okay, he begins to move.

We did away with condoms after my last period and I went to a doctor to be checked. He showed me his preseason results he always does and then condoms were a thing of the past. He feels even bigger without one and I cry out as the ridge of his head rubs against the deepest parts of me.

Good freaking gracious, he is incredible at this.

And oddly enough, the night ends exactly how he predicted.

With me screaming out I love him as I come, him following, and groaning the same back down my throat as he kisses me when he hits his climax.

EPILOGUE

JASON

PLAYOFFS ARE INSANE. And they're so damn long they feel like they take the same time as the entire season. Fortunately, our team kicks ass so we had a first round bye and an almost two break. Second round of playoffs began in mid April and we're now headed in to the first week of June. Two months of playoffs where fortunately, because we swept the second round against Buffalo in four games, we had a few days off before heading into round three against my brother Joey's team in Vegas.

That was a killer, all seven games, and every game was a hard-fought battle, so much so that it's been over a week since we beat Joey's team and he's still sending Jude and me shitty texts about cheering for Vancouver as we head into game six of the conference finals.

He's full of shit because obviously we know he's got our backs. Hell, he's even planning on being at the Stanley Cup finals against Dallas if we can get past these last two games.

Unfortunately, Vancouver had the early series lead and we're heading into game six with them still up by one game. Tonight could end it all. We lose, we're done.

And hell if I'm letting that happen. We're playing on fire. Our game is top notch. We're all healthy whereas Vancouver's star winger left last night's game early with an ankle injury and is still listed as unknown for tonight's game.

If he's out, we'll win no problem. While I like to claim I'm the best winger in the league, a close lead over Jude, Vancouver's winger, Tyler Markim, is the best damn player I've ever seen. I almost wish he wasn't injured so we could beat his team with him on the ice.

On the other hand, I'll happily take the win either way.

"You ready?" Tessa asks, curling her body against mine. She's naked beneath the covers and like always, her leg is thrown over mine. "How long have you been awake?"

"Not long." I run my hand up and down her back, wishing I could take care of us, take care of her before I have to head out. But today I need to keep my head in the game. "And yeah, I'm good." I turn and kiss her forehead. "Ready for tonight."

"Ready to win."

I grin. "Always. Hopefully."

"You will. You're the best."

"Damn straight. I'm going to get up, want to lay here and snooze or come have coffee with me?"

"Coffee. You. Always."

She groans as she shoves back the covers and stands. I get a view of her plump, gorgeous ass as she heads to the bathroom.

She never moved out of my apartment after deciding to stay in Charlotte. I let her think I'd allow it for a few weeks but when she kept touring apartments and coming back not liking anything, I told her that's because she was already home.

She agreed with a smile and a striptease and that night we moved all the things from the guest room closet into my room.

Then, I started looking for homes with a lot of space and more bedrooms than necessary so we can work on filling all of them.

We close on the monstrosity in a few weeks. I wanted to close immediately. Tessa wanted to wait until the season was over so we could do it together and not have the stress of constantly traveling added to moving.

As always when it comes to Tessa, she ended up getting her way. But that's mostly because I'll deny her nothing and if it means letting her move while she's relaxed, what fucking difference does it make to me?

It's close to where Sawyer and Debbie are looking, on lots of land where we're planning on putting in a pool sometime this summer once we finally move in.

I shove off the bed and tug on a pair of plaid pajama pants with the Ice Kings logo on my left hip.

I need coffee and food. Then I need a day of quiet to get my head in tonight's game.

I need to be ready. Because after tonight's game, I have a whole other game to win—getting Tessa to agree to marrying me.

THE LOCKER ROOM is tense heading into the third period. Outside, Sawyer is giving an interview to the news which I begged off doing. He's better at refocusing after interviews and tonight I can't afford any distractions other than the one already on my mind—

Proposing to Tessa as soon as I can.

"All right, listen up!" Coach Woods claps his hands, getting our attention. I've been pacing back and forth on my skates to stay warm and limber but as he shouts through our locker room in our own home arena, my feet still.

"Y'all have got this. I'm not going to fill your egos with all that fluffy and supportive shit some coaches do."

Around me, some of the players laugh. Coach is a good man, but definitely not a flowery one.

"So, I'm gonna say this and say this once so make sure you're listening. This team is the best damn team I've ever had the honor of coaching. You're brothers. You're family. Some of you closer than others." With that comment, his eyes skip to Jude and me and then Sawyer before he reveals a hint of a grin. If he can be this relaxed, it helps the rest of us.

The three of us tip our chins while a few guys slap our shoulders. It's all true. The Ice Kings are family. Which is why we're such a damn good team.

"Now, tighten up that third line, get the passes cleaner on the second. Take care of each other like the brothers you are, and I have no damn doubt we'll come out of this game tonight a winner and the game tomorrow headed to the finals. Fuck Markim being back tonight. We can take that fucker."

The locker room erupts in a series of Ooh-Raa's and Fuck Yeah's, and the coach throws his hand in the air, hand fisted.

We surround him, doing the same and once we're all gathered, the stench of our sweat co-mingling and overpowering, he shouts, "Ice Kings!"

To which we respond, "Victory!"

THREE HOURS LATER, I'm riding the high of the win, the final and game winning goal in the first overtime scored by me. Tessa has already ridden my dick, so damn excited to be headed into the final game tomorrow night she attacked me in my Escalade before we left the arena.

Thank God for the tinted windows so we weren't discovered. And Tessa's ability to bite down on her lip and whimper into my neck when she comes so hard I wasn't certain I could make the drive home.

But now we're here, tangled up in sheets, her head on my shoulder and while I should be calm and sated, I'm more worried about the next five minutes than I am the final game back in Vancouver in two days. That, I can control to a degree.

Tessa is always a freaking wildcard. One of the many reasons why I love her.

"Hey, got something for you to think about."

"Please don't tell me it's saltwater or not in the pool," she groans, burrowing her face into my chest.

I laugh and reach for the nightstand next to my side of the bed. I pull it open and dig out the ring box while she can't see. This isn't the most romantic way to propose, but I don't care. Better, I know Tessa won't.

"It's not about the pool."

"Curtains?"

"We've been over this. I don't give a shit about curtains or decor or rugs or whatever else you want to do to the house. I want the furniture large and comfortable and I get a say in television size. That's all I give a shit about."

"And the pool."

"And the pool," I concede. But only because I want it enormous with a floating area, a play area, a private hot tub area behind a waterfall. I want a water slide and a basketball hoop so we can make it as fun as possible for when we have kids or families over. "But I'm not talking about anything house-related."

I kiss the top of her head, smiling. I don't blame her. Hockey and houses is all we've talked about recently.

She pressed her hands to my chest and lifts up. As she does, I curl the ring box in my fist to hide it.

"What is it then?"

"I want you to think about something really important. It will involve planning. And I'll tell you right now... I'll do whatever you want."

"What am I planning? A party?"

"Close." I set the box on my stomach, popping the top so she can see the ring. "I was thinking our wedding."

She gapes at me. Jaw falls as she glances at the box. The enormous five-carat diamond princess cut ring sitting inside and then me. "Are you serious?"

I laugh at her expression, how she scrambles to her knees and grabs the box, shrieking again, "Are you freaking serious?"

"It's not fake," I say, teasing her about the ring.

I thought about waiting. It was less than a year ago she was engaged, but I feel like we've waited long enough. If she wants a long engagement, fine. She wants to elope after the game and head to Vegas, I'm all for it.

I tell her all of this while she stares at the ring and she grins at me, eyes wide and sparkling.

"Well, I do know how to make excellent travel plans."

I laugh, shaking my head at her and slip the ring from

the box. "I'll do whatever you want, Tessa, as long as you agree to marry me."

"Of course I'll marry you!"

She throws her arms around my shoulders and slams her mouth to mine. I slip the ring on her finger while I flip her to her back and it's an hour later where we're sweaty, done celebrating the first round of our engagement and Tessa is lying on her back, fiddling with her ring.

"I think I like the idea of Vegas," she says, turning to me. I'm propped on my side where I've been running my hand down her naked chest, tweaking her nipples here and there to get her slowly ready for the next round.

"Yeah?"

"I don't need anything big. And I like how small Sawyer and Debbie's was, but I don't really want to take the time to plan something."

She frowns and looks at me. "Is that, weird? That I don't want to plan a wedding?"

"Weird or not, I don't give a shit. I want us married, moving to our new home and starting a family and I want it all as soon as you're ready."

She kicks off the sheet that's been covering her waist, grabs my hand and slowly pushes it down her stomach to her thighs, before finding her slick and wet and already throbbing.

"Vegas," she whimpers as I slide two fingers inside of her. "I want to get married in Vegas and celebrate at The Luxor."

"Then that's what you'll get. Love you, Tessa. Always."

"I'll love you forever, Jason Taylor. I feel like I've always loved you."

I drag her to me so she's straddling my hips before I yank her down on my dick. She rides me to climax before I take my time getting there myself, driving her over the cliff twice before taking my own.

SEVENTY-TWO HOURS LATER, I've helped lead my team to another win and we're headed to Dallas to start the final series. But my greatest victory is the woman standing across from me in the small chapel, her hand in mine, and the sweet smile on her face as she says, "I do."

THANK YOU for reading Hooked On Her! Need more Ice Kings in your life? Be sure to sign up for my newsletter so you can stay up to date on more books in the series releasing this year.

www.staceylynnbooks.com

HARD CHECKED, book four in the Ice Kings series will release September 15th.

Pre-Order today: https://amzn.to/3kfe2MA

ACKNOWLEDGMENTS

HUGE thank you to Hilary and all of Social Butterfly PR for throwing your full enthusiasm and support behind each and every book I write. I have loved working with all of you and can't wait to see what's ahead! Hilary, I miss you most of all. ;-)

Ellie and Virginia, as always, thanks for putting up with my mess and spit-shining each manuscript until it sparkles. Thank you especially during this crazy time in our world for your flexibility and your extra hard work.

Shannon, you're the best. Always. Forever. Your talent is astounding and I'm thankful I can call you a friend.

Special, enormous thank you to my family who is always here, cheering me on and being so patient when I'm in my office. Your support is everything to me and I love you all with all of my heart.

To my Sweeties! I love you ladies and your excitement for my books! Special thanks to you this time for coming up with Brenna's name for me. It fits her perfectly.

To Lauren and Tamara – I'm so thankful our moves brought us into each other's lives!

To all the bloggers who devote their time and passion into reading books, book tours, release events, leaving reviews, promoting and pimping – you are all rockstars! Thank you for all the love over the years.

My family— I love you all to the moon and back. I don't know what I would do without you in my corner, cheering me on every step of the way.

And last but definitely not least – to you the reader. I'm blown away with every release how much you adore my books. You have made my dream a reality and I hope I can cheer you on with yours.

<u>**The Fireside Series**</u>

His to Love

His to Protect

His to Cherish

His to Seduce

<u>**Tangled Love Series**</u>

Entice

Embrace

Enflame

<u>**The Luminous Series**</u>

Dominate Me

Crave Me

Long For Me

<u>**Just One Series**</u>

Just One Song

Just One Week

Just One Regret

Just One Moment

<u>**The Nordic Lords Series**</u>

Point of Return

Point of Redemption

Point of Freedom

Point of Surrender